Judy Burgeson
1963

W9-BKA-366

THE MAN WITH TWO SHADOWS

By the same author

NOVELS : The Servant (1948)
           Line on Ginger (1949)
           The Rough and the Smooth (1951)
           Behind the Mirror (1955)

TRAVEL : Come to Dust (1945)
           Nomad (1947)
           Approach to Palestine (1947)
           North African Notebook (1948)
           Journey to Siwa (1950)

THE MAN WITH TWO SHADOWS

ROBIN MAUGHAM

HARPER & BROTHERS, PUBLISHERS, NEW YORK

THE MAN WITH TWO SHADOWS

Copyright © 1958 by Robin Maugham

Printed in the United States of America

All rights in this book are reserved.

No part of the book may be used or reproduced in any manner whatsoever without written permission except in the case of brief quotations embodied in critical articles and reviews. For information address Harper & Brothers 49 East 33rd Street, New York 16, N. Y.

The Library of Congress catalog entry for this book appears at the end of the text.

FOR
WINIFRED

THE MAN WITH TWO SHADOWS

I HAVE a full bottle of whisky and at least five hours before they come for me. I will write down the facts as best I can. That is my only hope.

*　　　　*　　　　*

The first time it happened for any dangerous length of time was on the day that I returned to Cairo in the winter of 1946.

The journey from England had been rough, and I remember I was glad to see the lights of the landing-strip at El Adem, our first stop in North Africa. While the plane was being refuelled I strolled away from the aerodrome, south towards the open. The darkness was lifting. I could see the first crimson threads of dawn streak the greyness of the sky to the east. I sniffed the dry, clean air which had swept freely across a thousand miles of desert, and I was glad to be back again.

Presently I walked into the Mess. I was thinking of the tank battles round El Adem and of those who had been killed, when suddenly I started. There were Germans close. I could hear their voices. I whipped round. Two blond German boys were talking to each other as they cleaned the tables for breakfast. One saw me staring at him and walked obediently towards me.

'Can I bring you something, sir?'

'What are you doing here?'

'We are prisoners and work on this aerodrome.'

The voice brought back disturbing memories. As I sat down my knees began to tremble and I could feel the sweat trickling down my sides. My right hand was touching the place on my head where the shrapnel had gone in. I made myself repeat the phrase they had taught me in hospital to use to calm myself: 'It's all over, and I'm well again.' I said this several times, like an incantation, and I soon felt better.

The sky was dappled with crimson and gold as the plane soared away from El Adem on the last lap to Cairo. I looked down at the desert where we fought. The broken tanks and trucks had been cleared away for scrap iron, and there were few traces of our fighting except the trenches and the graves. Then I made myself turn away from the past and concentrate on the mission ahead of me.

In London they thought I was visiting the Middle East as an ordinary free-lance journalist. But, in fact, General Maddern had secured me 'priority' and paid for my passage to Cairo for reasons of his own. As Chief Liaison Officer to our Middle East Bureau he wanted an unofficial observer—someone he could 'really trust', as he put it—to 'swan around and have a look-see'. He wanted me to travel round the Levant and then report back to him. I had served in his Division during the war; I had learned Arabic during the two years I had spent in various military hospitals before being invalided out of the Army. Moreover, I had been a student of Arab politics ever since I had read *Orientations* as an undergraduate; I had several Arab friends; I'd got over my head injury; being a professional journalist was a useful 'cover'; in fact, I was 'the very man'. Over port at the Travellers' Club Maddern's proposal had sounded fascinating, and I had accepted gladly. And now, as the plane droned over the desert, I was excited by the thought that I would be dining with him that very night. I decided that I would rest during the afternoon. It was all over, and I was well again, but I still had to be careful—especially in the job I'd taken on.

*   *   *

That evening I allowed myself plenty of time to change into my dinner-jacket and dressed slowly, savouring the joy of being back again in Cairo. Outside I could hear the familiar blare of horns above the dull roar of traffic. The room reserved for me was in the front of Shepheard's, which I had heard was the oldest section of the hotel. The floor quivered slightly when a heavy truck passed along the road beyond the terrace. But the thick yellow brocade curtains, the massive wardrobe and the large Empire desk looked impressively solid and enduring.

3

I finished the whisky-and-soda I had ordered from John's bar, I locked the door of my room, walked down the broad staircase into the hall, handed my key to the porter, stepped into a decrepit taxi which was waiting outside the terrace and gave the driver the address of General Maddern's house in Gezira. Then I opened the windows and smelled the acrid tang of Cairo while the taxi hooted its way through the crowded, dusty streets. At that moment I was excited, but my nerves were under control, and I had only had one drink all day.

As the taxi approached the General's house, the lights outside the portico were switched on so that the gravel drive was floodlit, and an orderly appeared in the doorway and saluted. He led me through the hall into a long white drawing-room. Standing at the far end of the room by a drinks-tray was a tall man in uniform, wearing the crowns of a Major. When he turned to greet me I recognised him. His name was Edward Pratt, and I had known him quite well during the war. He put down the cocktail-shaker and advanced towards me, grinning.

'Are you surprised?'

'Madly.'

'I rang you at Shepheard's, but they said you were having a doss.'

'Don't tell me you're Maddern's A.D.C.?'

'The appointment is of recent origin.'

'I'll bet it is,' I said, laughing.

Edward was a regular soldier who was very brave

and very lazy. His services were not appreciated in peace-time.

'You be careful, Peter, or you won't get a daiquiri,' he said. 'And I made it specially for you. I take it you *are* allowed to drink?'

'Heavens, yes.'

'Splendid. The boss is winging his way back from seeing Ibn Saud in Riyadh and they've just 'phoned through to say his plane's delayed, so we've plenty of time. What's new in London? How's that attractive girl I saw you dancing with at the Four Hundred? Wasn't her name Joanna something?'

'She's all right,' I said.

Joanna was one of the reasons I had accepted Maddern's offer. Two months previously she had come round to my flat at midnight to tell me she was in love with a married man. She would marry him when his divorce came through. I was trying to forget her.

'I can see I'd better try another tack,' Edward said. 'How much did you manage to rook them for your flat?'

*　　　*　　　*

We must have been gossiping for about twenty minutes when the double doors at the end of the room opened and two Brigadiers came in. They were both stout and red-faced, and the larger one moved in a curiously constricted manner, as if he wore corsets.

5

'The General will be here in a minute,' the stouter one announced. 'He's washing his hands.'

When Edward introduced me, I realised from what he had said that they must be the General's two assistants. Edward had referred to them as Tweedledum and Tweedledee. I was trying to make polite conversation when an orderly flung open the double doors, and General Maddern appeared. He took six paces into the room and then stopped still for an instant, as if examining the group we made round the drinks-table.

He was a small, lean man in his early fifties, with a clean-shaven rather boyish face, round blue eyes and curly grey hair. He was not impressive to look at. Yet as he stood looking towards us, motionless and intent, I could feel the strength of his personality flowing through me like a current.

Suddenly he threw back his head and smiled. .

'Good evening, gentlemen,' he said. His voice was soft but crisp. Then he crossed the room and shook my hand.

'How are you, Peter? I'm glad you made it. You look perfectly fit. I believe that shrapnel did you good. Gave you a rest for a while. Has Edward been looking after you properly?'

'Yes. Thank you, sir.'

'Edward, where's my whisky-and-soda? Thank you. I told them we wouldn't eat for another fifteen minutes. His Majesty gave me far too much to eat and nothing whatever to drink. The old rascal can produce whisky when he feels like it, but he's as tricky as they're made.

And nothing disconcerts him. There was a scuffling noise behind the curtains at one end of the conference tent, and I looked up to see a slave hurrying off a young girl who had obviously crept in to have a look-see. The King stared me straight in the face and then spoke to the interpreter, who translated the King's words thus: "His Majesty says he spent his youth in wars depopulating his country, so that it is only right he should spend his old age repopulating it." '

The two Brigadiers laughed loudly. Maddern took my arm quickly, as if the noise of the laughter hurt him.

'Let's sit down quietly and talk shop,' he said, and moved towards the sofa near the windows.

Up to that moment I can recollect almost every word and gesture—almost every detail of the evening. And after we had sat down on the sofa I can remember Maddern saying to me: 'Now, Peter, tell me, what do your Arab friends in London think of this Arab League business?'

While I paused before replying I can remember looking down at his hands, which were lying motionless on his knees. The tips of his fingers were broad and the nails well manicured. Then, as I stared down at his hands, what I can only describe as a curtain came down over my mind, and I remembered—and still can remember—nothing more until I woke up the following morning.

*   *   *

7

At first I did not know where I was. Then I saw the light filtering through the faded yellow curtains, and I realised I was in my bed in Shepheard's. But what had happened? Then with a sickening lurch I remembered arriving at the General's house, feeling tired and nervous, drinking several cocktails, sitting down on the sofa, listening to his question. And then . . . What then? I could recollect nothing beyond that moment. But I could guess what had happened. If only I had fainted— 'passed clean out', as Edward would have put it, the harm could be mended. But what I was almost certain had happened was something more shaming and alarming. I had had a recurrence of the 'black-outs' which had confined me to the Hospital for Head Injuries at Oxford for nearly a year.

After I had been invalided back from the Middle East because of my head wound, I had begun to lose consciousness for short periods of time. For instance, I might be talking with a friend in his flat, when a curtain would come down over my mind—like a shutter over the lens of a camera—and I would remember nothing until it lifted, perhaps when I was saying goodbye, perhaps when I was walking home. The friend would have noticed nothing unusual. In the Hospital for Head Injuries I was told that these 'black-outs'—a loathsome expression, but no worse than 'fugues' or 'bouts of retrogressive amnesia', as the doctors sometimes called it—were the result of my head wound and would gradually grow less frequent and in time stop altogether. When I accepted Maddern's offer I had not had

8

an attack for over six months. And now, my very first night in Cairo, the wretched thing had happened again.

My mouth felt dry. I drank a glass of water. At that moment I saw my clothes. They were lying in an untidy heap on the Recamier sofa—an old tweed suit I had brought out to wear in the desert and had left at the bottom of my suitcase, a flannel shirt, a brown tie. I got out of bed and opened the wardrobe. My dinner-jacket was hanging on a clothes-hanger. I lay down again in bed and tried to think. Obviously, I had come back to the hotel and changed out of my dinner-jacket into the tweed suit. Why? To go out in the town? Probably. My dinner-jacket would have been very conspicuous. But why had I gone out again? To meet an Arab who could give me information? Perhaps. To wander round the brothel quarter? Possibly—but unlikely. On leave from the Western Desert I had once or twice been round the more famous brothels, but drunk and elated as I was, I had been depressed by the sight of the young prostitutes and disgusted by the older ones.

I looked towards the table beside my bed. My engagement book was lying on top of my wallet. I knew that when I had left the hotel the previous evening I had ten Egyptian pounds. My taxi to Gezira had cost forty piastres or so. Allowing for a taxi back I should have at least nine pounds left. I took the notes out of my wallet. There were only four pounds.

After my previous black-outs I had sometimes found a note or an address scribbled on a slip of paper which

9

had given me a clue where I had been or what I had done. I looked in my engagement book. I turned to the date, December 17th. And there I found written clearly and firmly in my own handwriting:

'Take Colonel Parry to see G. M. at 11 a.m.'

Parry was Deputy Chief of Intelligence to the Middle East Bureau. G. M. must be General Maddern. Why should I ever have supposed I should take Parry, whom I scarcely knew, to see Maddern?

The telephone by my bed had started ringing. I lifted the receiver. It was Edward.

'How are *you* this morning?' he asked.

I was determined not to confess my weakness unless I was forced to, so I hedged.

'Exhausted,' I said.

'I'm not surprised.'

I decided to bluff.

'How do you think things went?' I asked.

He paused. Then he said: 'Well, you were very outspoken. At one moment I thought that my great white chief was going to turf you out. But to the amazement of all he took it like a lamb—though I warn you. Don't try it on twice, and don't forget you're supposed to be turning up at the office at eleven pronto with that old slug Parry.'

'So that's still on?' I said.

'Why shouldn't it be? It was your bright idea, wasn't it? Incidentally, would you like to lunch with me afterwards?'

'I'd love to.'

'Fine. Let's meet at John's bar at about one-thirty. But I'll be there to welcome you at the office. Eleven ack emma. Don't be late.'

I looked at my watch. It was ten o'clock. While I shaved I tried to see the funny side of it. Here I was—committed to bring two important British officials together—and I hadn't a notion for what reason. But though I managed to smile, my hands were still trembling. If I was forced to confess about my black-outs I knew my mission would be cancelled, and I was desperately keen to carry out my assignment. First, I believed that I would find out more than the usual type of Intelligence Officer who spent his time sitting behind a desk devouring reports from unreliable agents. Secondly, Maddern had promised to provide transport and pay for my expenses. I could never have afforded the trip otherwise. Before the war I had studied for the Bar. My head wound had made me forget the little law I knew. Then my father died, leaving me a small income which was just sufficient to let me take up the career of a free-lance journalist. I had enough to live on. What I made from articles and a few short stories helped me to pay for occasional trips abroad. At the age of thirty I was starting in a new profession. I could never earn enough money to pay for the tour that Maddern wanted me to make, and no newspaper would be prepared to send out an inexperienced reporter. Lastly, my long-range plan was to make myself an expert in Middle East affairs so that eventually I could get the job of correspondent on the staff of one of the few responsible newspapers. For these three reasons I dare not let anyone know about my black-out the previous evening.

*   *   *

I took deep breaths to calm myself as I walked along the corridor to Colonel Parry's office in G.H.Q. I found him seated rigidly behind his desk, his knees pressed close together, his back erect, stomach drawn in, chest thrown out, and his face pointing straight ahead, as if he were sitting to attention. He was a plump, middle-aged man, with a small black moustache and an amazingly pale complexion. Thin strands of black hair were plastered back carefully over his head to disguise the bald patches. But although his hair looked greasy I noticed there was scurf on his collar. Perhaps that was why he was going bald.

'Peter Grant, isn't it?' he said. 'In the Crendon Yeomanry, weren't you?'

'That's right.'

'But now you're in civvy street, I gather.'

'Yes.'

'I was told you'd be coming round to report to me. We've an appointment with General Maddern at eleven. Now do you mind telling me just what it's all about?'

I did not hesitate. I had been expecting that question.

'If you don't mind, I'd rather wait until we meet the General,' I said, rather smugly.

At that stage I could only play for time and hope

that something would happen to remind me what had been in my mind when I suggested the meeting. At the worst I was determined to invent a reason.

Parry frowned, then forced his lips to smile. He got up stiffly.

'In that case I suppose we might as well push along,' he said, and opened the door for me, and together we passed through his ante-room and walked out into the corridor. As we crossed over to the block occupied by Maddern and his staff I could feel the sweat, cold beneath my arms.

Edward Pratt received us cheerfully in the outer office. His desk was half covered with telephones. The only paper on it was *The Times*. Glancing down I saw that he had almost finished the crossword puzzle. Maddern had probably chosen him for his imperturbable good humour. Unlike me he never panicked.

'The General's expecting you both,' he said. 'Come right in.'

He opened the door leading to the General's room, ushered us in, and withdrew smartly. Maddern was sitting on the edge of his desk, looking up at a vast map of the Middle East which filled the whole wall behind. For an instant he did not move. Once again I was amazed that a man could be so motionless and yet so alert. His stillness was like that of a leopard before it springs. Then he turned and smiled at us.

'Good morning, gentlemen,' he said, and pushed a heavy silver cigarette-box towards us.

'Sit yourselves down and help yourselves to

cigarettes. Haven't seen you at the Club for some time, Parry. How's the wife?'

'Better, thank you, sir.'

'Glad to hear it. You must both of you come and dine with me one night. I'll get Edward to fix it. I wish I could persuade my wife to come out, but she positively refuses to leave the children.'

This was untrue, and Parry probably knew it. Lady Maddern was a pleasant dowdy woman who lived in a small village in Wiltshire. Maddern preferred her out of the way. There was a young Swiss girl he kept in a flat near Giza.

'By the way, Parry,' Maddern was saying. 'You haven't by any chance got a signed photograph of Monty, have you?'

Parry was surprised, but long training made him disguise the fact.

'I don't think so,' he said cautiously.

'I've got to find one. You see, last time he was out here, Monty gave me a signed photograph—cabinet size or whatever it's called—and after he'd gone I put it away in some drawer, and now we just can't find it. And the man's coming to dine with me on Thursday. You do see the fix I'm in.'

'Perhaps the Embassy could help,' Parry suggested.

'If they can't I must ring up Paget.' He pronounced it Pagé. 'He's sure to have one.'

As he spoke, Maddern glanced down at Parry and must have noticed the scurf on his collar, for his nose wrinkled in distaste.

14

'Well, I suppose we'd better stop coffee-housing and get down to business,' he said. 'Supposing you kick-off, Peter?'

The moment I had been dreading had come. I longed for a cigarette, but I knew my hands would shake as I lit it. Both men were looking at me. I said the only thing I could think of.

'I'd rather you started the ball rolling, sir.'

The cliché softened my refusal to begin.

'But it's your proposal, not mine. And you're here to sell us the idea.'

'I know, sir. But I'd rather you started, just the same.'

For an instant I thought Maddern would be angry. Then he put his hands down on to his desk and rested them on a long white ruler and turned to Parry.

'Very well,' he said. 'Now this is the form.'

He got up, holding the ruler, and walked briskly towards the map.

'Of the countries we can consider as forming the fertile crescent,' he began—and the tip of his ruler described an arc embracing the Lebanon, Syria, Jordan and Iraq—'we know perfectly well there is only one country that is unreliable.'

At that moment it came back to me. I still could remember nothing of what had happened after Maddern's question the previous night. But I could guess—almost certainly—the plan I must have put forward later that evening. It had been at the back of my mind for the last six months.

'Over to you, Peter,' Maddern was saying.

15

'It may not work,' I said. 'But at the worst it could do no harm. My idea is that if I went first to Damascus . . .'

I looked up at Maddern's face, and I knew that I had guessed right. I was saved.

*   *   *

I left G.H.Q. at twelve-thirty and took a taxi to a shop near Groppi's where they made better desert-boots than you could get anywhere in London. I then strolled happily through the streets, arriving back at Shepheard's towards half-past one. As I was walking through the hall towards John's bar I remembered for some reason the story I had been told about the long red carpet which stretched from end to end of the hotel. During the Armistice Day celebrations at the end of the First World War, some young officers had seized the manager of Shepheard's, folded him up in the carpet at the garden end, and rolled him out into the street at the other. The man had nearly died of shock. Since then, it was said, the carpet was divided into short stretches.

I was crossing the circular lobby where Cairenes could be seen sitting at little tables sipping tea or coffee at almost any hour, when I noticed a slim, dark man who was sitting by himself. With his thick black hair and rather fleshy nose he looked more like a Syrian than an Egyptian. I noticed him because as I passed him it seemed to me that he raised his hand in a gesture of recognition. I turned round to see if the signal was intended for someone following close behind me. No-one else was crossing the lobby. I turned back to the Syrian, but he was no longer looking at me. His attention was absorbed by a thick signet ring which he wore on the little finger of his left hand. With his right hand he was sliding it up and down the length of his finger. I decided that I must have imagined his gesture, or perhaps he was beckoning to a waiter on the far side of the room. I walked on towards the bar. I still do not understand why I should have shuddered.

*　　　*　　　*

At the end of a happy lunch with Edward, I felt sufficiently strong to put the question I had been longing to ask.

'Did you think I was very outspoken last night?'

'Well, you did lay down the law a bit.'

'When did you first notice I was getting a bit above myself?'

He looked at me sharply.

'Don't tell me you can't remember?'

'Of course I can remember. I just wondered how it struck you, that's all.'

'We were both fairly high, but I didn't realise how far gone you were till we sat down to eat.'

'I was drunk. Why not say it?'

'No. That's the odd part of it. You weren't drunk. If you don't mind me saying so, you made more sense than you usually do. But you were over-confident—you used a lot of slang words you'd never have dared use sober —and you were pretty indiscreet, though not half as indiscreet as my boss was later on when he got going.'

'Did he realise I was high?'

'I expect so. But he didn't seem to mind. He seems quite fond of you. I can't think why.'

*   *   *

After lunch I went upstairs to have a siesta. I unlocked the door of my room and walked in. Propped up against the mirror of the dressing-table was a long, thick envelope. On it my name PETER GRANT was written in block letters with a blunt pencil. So I opened it.

Inside was a bundle of greasy one-pound Egyptian notes.

*   *   *

I counted the notes—as if the number of them could give me some explanation. There were exactly two hundred. I rang for the suffragi and asked him if he had seen anyone come into my room. He had seen no-one. I asked the hall porter if an envelope had been delivered to him to be sent up to my room. He knew nothing about it.

Who could possibly have sent me two hundred pounds? Not Maddern. After Parry had left us that morning he had arranged for me to be paid the first instalment of my expenses. Had I been to some club and gambled during my black-out? The Mohammed Ali was the only gambling club I knew, and I would not have changed out of my dinner-jacket to go there. And why the block letters? Why the anonymity? Then I remembered the Syrian in the lobby who had half raised his hand as I passed. But why should he have delivered two hundred pounds to my room?

Once or twice while on leave during the war, I had played roulette or chemin-de-fer at a private party in some houseboat on the Nile that had been hired for the evening. Perhaps while I was roaming round the town I had met someone I knew and had been taken to some private gambling party. But I could not afford to play for high stakes. How could I ever have won two hundred pounds, and why should the money be delivered to me so secretly?

Suddenly I felt tired and sick. I undressed and got into bed and threw back the blankets. As I lay back against the pillows, I remembered the long months in the Hospital for Head Injuries, and I decided that I would gladly suffer attacks of nausea and occasional black-outs rather than face again the interminable tests and examinations and questions by kind neurologists and well-meaning psychiatrists. I could not endure to be told yet once more the patiently deduced explanation of my amnesia. I could have told them long before they

19

started analysing me. I knew the reason, and I knew that as long as I lived I would never forget.

Even now, when I closed my eyes, I knew I would see the tanks spread out like chequers over the desert, and I would feel the heat of noon—so strong that we could scarcely breathe. Ken's light cotton shirt and shorts were black with sweat as he crawled out of the driver's seat. They clung to his body like a thin, wet bathing-dress.

'There's not enough water to brew-up,' I said, 'but at least we've got an hour's rest.'

Ken nodded and parted his cracked lips in a smile and flung himself down in the few yards of shade on the far side of the tank, where the rest of the crew joined him. I unstrapped a blanket and laid it out in a thin strip of shade by the off-side tracks. But as the sun moved across the hot, white sky the area of protection diminished and then was gone. Presently through a haze of weariness I heard Ken's voice.

'Why don't you change places with me, sir? Then you'd be in the shade.'

'Doesn't matter. I'm all right here. Thanks all the same.'

I felt wonderfully sleepy.

I was awakened by a deafening roar, growing louder and louder. I sprang to my feet. Then the roar was pierced by the staccato cracks of cannon-fire. I felt a fierce blow on my head. I stumbled against the side of the tank. The noise moved rapidly away. In a great silence I heard the patter of liquid falling on to sand,

and then a horrible moaning noise. I looked round. Something was staggering slowly towards me. The head had been split open and half the face hung down, flopping with blood. From the dark curly hair I knew it was Ken.

I can remember nothing more until I was being lifted into the ambulance, and they told me he was dead. That was over an hour later. I had blacked out because of shock—because I could not endure the anguish of his death. My subsequent black-outs were a form of escape from a situation or memory that my subconscious found unbearable. It was as easy as that. But it was all over now, and I was well again—or nearly well, and the following day I would go to Damascus.

I would not report the incident of the pound notes to General Maddern, for I could not do so without telling him of my disability. But I would not use the two hundred pounds.

I got up from the bed and locked the notes in my suitcase.

That evening I dined quietly with some Arab friends at a café near the Semiramis and went early to bed.

*   *   *

I had no black-out of any kind for the next six months, and I was well and quite happy, and Maddern was pleased with my reports. But my fertile crescent plan failed—mainly, I am convinced, because of the ignorance and timidity of the officials with whom I had to deal. For the first time I became aware of the ineptness of our Foreign Service. Since the invention of the telephone and cable, almost every one of our diplomats abroad has been chained to his desk by signals and papers from Whitehall. He has little time to get to know a foreign people, and his every action is checked and controlled by London, so that he loses initiative. He no longer needs to be resourceful; he needs to be an efficient clerk. And a different type begins to be chosen for the Service. . . . But it has all been said before and better by the few experts who really do know, and no-one has listened to them, and now it's too late. We've lost the Middle East. . . .

But in those early days there was still hope, and I honestly believe that in my small way I helped Maddern in his struggle to persuade the Foreign Office that in dealing with Arabs individuals are more important than policies, actions more important than words.

The day after I returned to Cairo in June, I found that Edward was away on leave, but his deputy told me that the General wished me to lunch with him the following day. When I arrived, a little late, at Maddern's house, I was disappointed to find a lunch party. The two Brigadiers were there—redder than ever in the intense summer heat. There was an aggressively Zionist labour politician with his extremely attractive and well-dressed wife, and the Lebanese Minister and his wife, who had been invited to meet them. I prattled as brightly as I could with the politician's wife, and wondered if I would get a chance of talking to Maddern.

But when, after coffee and liqueurs, the guests rose to go, he beckoned me to stay behind, and the deputy A.D.C. left us alone together.

Maddern sank back into an armchair and fanned himself with a silk handkerchief.

'Sometimes I think I'll give it all up and go and farm in Rhodesia,' he said. 'They won't listen to a word I say. The C.-in-C.'s all right. But what can he do? The Embassy boys won't budge. They drive me simply mad.'

'They're scared to take any definite action.'

'They're scared, period. And now the balloon's going to go up in North Africa. Just mark my words.'

Suddenly he leaned forward.

'Peter, are you still free to work for us?'

I felt a stab of excitement.

'Yes.'

'Then this is what I suggest. Go up to Alex for a short holiday. You look a bit run down. You'll find Edward there. He can put you up in his flat. But no pub-crawling. I want you fit. I want you to make a long journey from the frontier of Egypt right along the Med to the Atlantic coast of Morocco. I want you to find out just what's happening in the six Arab lands between. Take your time. I've got a fund that can pay all your expenses. I'll be flying up to Alex next week. I'll give you further details then.'

*   *   *

That evening I sat on the terrace of the Mena House Hotel dining alone. During the last six months I had had to meet so many different people that to be alone was a luxury. Besides, I wanted to relish my happiness at the prospect of another trip. I reckoned I would now be living in Arab countries for at least another year, and already the shape of a book I might write was forming in my mind. I sipped my wine and stared at the moonlight over the Pyramids and the desert pale and sparkling beyond. I should add, for the sake of accuracy, that the glass of wine was the first drink I had had all day.

A tall Sudanese suffragi in a flowing white galabieh came up to me. He bowed and smiled.

'*Gahwa, ya sidi?*' he asked. 'Coffee, sir?'

I noticed that his nose had been broken and that his teeth were very white.

'*Gahwa, ya sidi?*' he repeated softly, and the curtain fell down over my mind.

*   *   *

I was lying naked in bed on a hard mattress. I was staring up at an oil-lamp that hung from the ceiling and cast strange shadows over the rough, whitewashed walls of the little room. Below the lamp was a table with a pitcher of water and a basin on it—and a grimy towel. I felt dazed and sick. Then I heard a faint rustle on the mattress beside me. I turned round. A young girl was looking at me with large black eyes. She was naked except for a dirty cotton brassière which covered her small breasts. She wore no make-up. From her body I reckoned she might just have been fifteen. She was very slender with a tawny-coloured skin that seemed to glisten in the lamp-light. As I turned she spoke.

'Why are you like this tonight, Tommy?' she asked. 'Are you not glad to see me?'

I could think of nothing to say, but I smiled at her. Then she put her arm round my shoulder and pressed herself against me and began to stroke the back of my neck. Her skin was very smooth. She did not use any scent, and her body had the acrid tang of the Cairo streets. I took her face between my hands and kissed her. Immediately, she pressed her mouth against mine and parted her lips while her hands caressed me, brushing lightly against my skin. For a moment she lifted her face away from me.

'I do love you, Tommy,' she said. 'I am grateful to you, and I do love you.'

Suddenly I longed to see her breasts. I felt there was something obscene about taking her while her breasts were covered. Moving slowly and gently I put both my hands on her brassière and slipped it off. Even as I touched the stiff cotton, her hands flew up to cover her breasts. With another quick movement she twitched the brassière into position. But what I had already seen made me want to retch with disgust. Her nipples were encircled by dozens of small sores about a quarter of an inch in diameter. Some were half-healed, others were red and inflamed.

25

The girl was looking up at me. Was it fear or reproach in her wide, dark eyes?

'I told you that you must not see again,' she said. 'It is bad for you to see. When you come to me next they will be gone.'

There was a knock at the door.

'Ageyle!' It was a woman's raucous voice. 'Ageyle!'

There was menace in the abrupt tone. The girl moved away from me.

'Now it is too late,' she said in a whisper. 'If you stay more long she will suspect. You must put on your clothes and go.'

For an instant I hesitated. Then I kissed her forehead and got up from the bed and dressed. I felt sorry for her. She looked so young and small.

'Isn't there anything I can do to help?' I said.

She stared at me wildly.

'Are you mad?' she whispered. 'Have you forgotten? This time you are not drunk. What is wrong in you tonight?'

'You must let me help you.'

'Tommy, what is it? Please tell me you do not forget. Please tell me. Tell me quick.'

She was desperate. I knew that I must help her. There was a louder knock at the door.

'Ageyle!' the raucous voice shouted.

'*Isra'a. Al rajul yintathrak.*' 'The man is waiting for you. Hurry.'

'Please tell me,' the girl repeated. She was breathing heavily and trembling.

26

I tore a page from my engagement book and wrote down my name and room number at Shepheard's.

'Listen,' I said. 'Bring this round to Shepheard's—any time tomorrow morning—and I'll do what I can to help you.'

'Do I not know your name? Tommy Grant at Shepheard's Hotel. Have I not promised to send word to you when they have fetched me away from here? Put that paper in your pocket, or she will find it and suspect.'

Again there was a knock at the door.

'Ageyle! Ta'al Ageyle!'

'You must go,' she whispered.

I pulled out my wallet. I had about half a dozen pounds in it. I took them and pressed them into her hands.

'No,' she whispered. 'Only one pound to me or she will suspect.'

'You can hide the rest.'

She looked round the bare room.

'Where can I hide anything so she will not find it?'

She put a pound on the table by the bed and handed me back the other notes.

'Ageyle! Ageyle!'

'Tell me you have not forgotten,' she said.

'I'll see you at Shepheard's.'

'Yes. If you do not forget.'

'I won't forget.'

'I love you, Tommy. Please remember.'

'Goodnight,' I said. 'I'll remember.'

I walked out into an ill-lit corridor with three doors

27

leading off it. There was no sound from the rooms. I clambered down a narrow wooden staircase into a small room which was lit by an Aladdin lamp with a paper shade. A large fat woman in a pink evening dress was sitting on a divan surrounded by worn silk cushions that were smeared with brown stains. Her heavy jowls were covered with a thick layer of powder. The whiteness of her face contrasted with the angry red of her thick arms which bulged out of her short sleeves. She did not look up as I came in.

'How much did you give her?' she asked.

'One pound.'

'That is correct. Now you give me two pounds.' Her accent was vaguely French.

'Give,' she said.

I handed her the money. I wondered if there was any point in talking to her about Ageyle. But as I watched her pull out her handbag from under the cushions and tuck in the notes, I felt a sudden revulsion. I only wanted to escape from her presence. I walked quickly towards the nearest door and flung it open.

'Not that door. Come back,' she cried. 'Come back immediately. There is the door out.' She pointed to a door the other side of the staircase.

But I had looked into the other room. An Egyptian of about sixty, wearing a tarboosh and a green gaberdine suit, was sitting on the back of a chair smoking a cigarette in a jade holder. His eyes were fixed on his cigarette, as if the glowing end of it hypnotised him. He was very lean, with a thin face and grey hair and a

28

delicate, aquiline nose. He would have looked ascetic had it not been for the thick, pale lips jutting out from his face. After I had opened the door he slowly removed his gaze from his cigarette and looked up at me from his trance. Then he turned away quickly.

'This door,' the woman was shouting. 'And next time be more careful.'

I crossed the room, opened the far door and walked out into a dark hallway. By the glow of the rush-lights on the floor I could see two suffragis lying on a straw mat. They shuffled to their feet as I appeared and held out their hands for a tip, and I gave them some small change. They were both tall and heavily-built. I supposed the fat woman must have chosen them for their size.

I walked out into the street and turned the corner. Then I stopped. I had no idea where I was. From the dingy houses and an occasional villa with peeling walls and an allotment behind it, I reckoned I was on the out-skirts of Giza. But until you get to know a town well, one street can look very much like another. I lit a cigarette. There was a faint breeze, and the flame from the short wax match burnt my finger. At that moment I remembered where I had once before seen a small sore about a quarter of an inch in diameter. It had been on Edward's wrist the day after he had made a drunken bet with an officer he disliked. The bet had been that he could hold a lighted cigarette to his wrist longer than his opponent.

I was still standing at the corner of the house. Then

from the room above I heard a scream of pain which ended in a gasp as if it had been stifled. I looked up and saw that there was a heavy iron grille over the window. And then I knew the reason for the sores on Ageyle's breasts; I knew the reason why the Egyptian had been staring at his cigarette. There was a low moan from the window above. I could bear it no longer. I rushed round the corner. The door of the house was locked. I beat with my fists against it. The door was opened by one of the suffragis. I brushed past him and flung open the door leading into the inner room. The fat woman was lying on the sofa. The other suffragi was kneeling beside her, and he was naked. When she saw me she pushed him away and tried to stand up.

'Get out, you English bastard,' she screamed. 'Get out.'

Again I heard a moan of pain. I ran to the staircase, but as I put my foot on the first step the suffragi from the hall caught hold of my shoulder. I tore myself loose, but his other hand had fastened on my arm, and he pulled me back and pinioned me. Then the naked one crossed over to me. He was sweating and breathing heavily. I saw his fist shoot out, and I tried to move. I felt the blow crash against my forehead, and I lost consciousness.

*　　　*　　　*

The sun was glinting across the desert. My head was aching, and there was a taste of blood in my mouth. At first I thought I was lying in the sand beside my tank. Then I remembered. I stumbled to my feet and looked round. Fifty yards to the north a metalled road ran like a dusty ribbon over the plain. On the horizon to the west I could see the control tower of an aerodrome and behind it a tall mosque. Then I knew where I was. They had dumped me in a stretch of waste land beyond Heliopolis.

I limped towards the road. I must have bruised my leg when I fell. My lip was cut open, my head throbbed painfully, and my wristwatch and wallet had been stolen. I decided that the damage might have been far worse. My anxiety was for Ageyle. She knew where I was staying. Could she not escape from them? Or was she guarded like a prisoner, night and day? Why had she said to me: 'This time you are not drunk'? Had I visited her that first night in Cairo after I dined with Maddern? When else could I have seen her? And why did she keep saying 'Have you forgotten? Please do not forget'? What could I have promised—except to help her if she came to see me at the hotel? Where had the brothel been? How could I ever find the street again?

The last thing I could remember before I had blacked out after dinner was the Sudanese suffragi at Mena House. Could he have been a link with the brothel? Possibly. Yet it was almost certain I had been to the brothel once before.

I got a lift from a passing truck. An hour later I was back in my room at Shepheard's. I telephoned to George

31

Hassoun, a Lebanese friend of mine who worked in the Secretariat of the Arab League. He came round to see me at eleven that morning, and I explained the events of the previous night, without mentioning my black-out. I said that I had been taken to the brothel in a taxi when I was drunk, and I did not even know what district the street was in. George played with the ice in his glass of Pernod, and occasionally nodded his large, round, white face in agreement to show that he was listening. We were sitting on the terrace of Shepheard's, watching the street in case Ageyle should be afraid to come into the hotel. When it was noon and Ageyle had not appeared, George took me to see a Colonel he knew in the Police. For an hour I described the street, the detached house, Ageyle, the fat woman, the slim Egyptian and the two suffragis as best I could. The Colonel was pathetically anxious to help, but he could offer little hope.

'The fact that they did not kill you means they were intending to move house,' he said. 'Perhaps other people had heard the screams. If you telephone me later this evening I may have news for you. But I doubt it.'

At six I drove out to the Mena House Hotel and sat down at a table on the terrace in the bright sunshine. Three or four suffragis were chattering together under the awning. After I had sat down for a minute or so one of them left the group and approached me. It was the suffragi who had offered me coffee the previous night.

'*Masa al khayr, ya sidi.*' 'Good evening, sir.'

'Good evening.'

'What can I bring you, sir?'

'A long whisky-and-soda.'

'*Hadir, ya sidi.*'

He bowed, and turned to go.

'Wait a moment,' I said; '*Ismak ayhu?*' 'What's your name?'

'Suleiman.' His voice was deep and gentle.

'How long have you worked here?'

'Since the end of the war, ya sidi.'

I saw that he was looking at my swollen lip and bruised forehead.

'Last night, ya sidi,' he began, and then stopped.

'Yes? What were you going to say?'

'Did you have an accident?'

'Yes,' I said. 'Did you hear about it?'

'No, ya sidi. Was it in a taxi?'

'Why do you ask?'

'Because when you leave last night you say you will walk for a while and then take a taxi.'

I looked at him carefully. His large eyes met my gaze with calm innocence. I was now convinced that he had nothing to do with the brothel. As I watched him I noticed that a thin scar ran from his frizzy black hair in a straight line to the bridge of his nose.

'Where did you get that scar?'

'In the war, ya sidi. I was in the Sudanese Defence Force.'

He smiled at me shyly and bowed and walked away. I drank the whisky-and-soda he brought me, left him a large tip and drove back into Cairo to meet George.

At eight o'clock we telephoned the Colonel at his home. He had no news and sounded despondent.

'They may even have moved to another town,' he said.

George was a Christian, so he could drink with a good conscience. That night we went out and got drunk together. I knew I would have a black-out, but I did not care. I only wanted to forget that moan of pain.

I remember unlocking the door of my room in Shepheard's when I returned about midnight that evening; I can remember nothing more until I woke up in bed the next morning.

*   *   *

I looked round the room. The clothes I had worn the previous night were hung neatly on a chair. I counted the pound notes in the new wallet I had bought. There should have been about half a dozen left; there were in fact seven. I decided that my black-out had been entirely due to my drunkenness and that nothing unusual had happened. When I had dressed I telephoned the Colonel. There was still no news.

'It is possible that I might be able to trace the man in the green gaberdine suit,' he said. 'But if I have him brought in for questioning he will lie. And what can we prove? You can give evidence that you saw him in a brothel. But what more?'

34

It was important news that we might be able to trace the Egyptian with the jade holder. I rang George Hassoun and repeated what the Colonel had said.

'Can you find me some good detective agency?' I asked. 'Is there such a thing in Cairo?'

'I should imagine so. Why?'

'If we can trace the Egyptian, we can have him followed. He may lead us to Ageyle.'

'That's quite an idea,' George said. 'I'm not free till this evening. But I'll meet you at nine with the answer to your question.'

A detective agency would probably be expensive. I unlocked the suitcase where I had kept the two hundred greasy one-pound notes in the same long envelope, hidden in the inside pocket of a leather jacket. For some reason—perhaps superstitiously—I had been unwilling to use them. But now I felt free to spend them. I took out the jacket and felt in the pocket. There was no envelope. I searched the other pockets; I went through the other clothes in the suitcase. The money had gone. But the suitcase had been locked, and the only key— which was of an unusual shape—was on a ring I always carried with me.

*   *   *

That day I lunched with some English friends on Gezirah and went to the club to swim and stayed on for drinks, so I did not return to my room at Shepheard's until a quarter to nine. Propped against the mirror of the dressing-table was a long white envelope with my name written in capitals with a pencil. At first I thought it was the envelope that had contained the money. Then I saw that it was flat and uncreased. As I picked it up I wondered if I should find there was not even a letter inside it. Perhaps it was some cruel joke played by the person who had stolen the money. I ripped open the envelope. Inside was a small piece of white paper. On it, written in capitals, but in a different hand, and with a red pencil, were five words:

AGEYLE SAYS THANKYOU TO TOMMY.

*   *   *

My fingers are getting stiff from writing. I have just had a break and my second whisky today. I've at least another three hours before they come for me.

Reading through these last pages I am surprised I did not guess the truth. But you must remember that I had checked up with various friends who had been with me during my black-outs and they had noticed no sudden change in me. In fact, they were unaware that I *had* blacked out. Moreover, these bouts of retrogressive amnesia were not as frequent as reading my narrative, which is only concerned with them, might suggest. I only had three attacks during those seven months. Even so, I realised that I might well be a 'poor security risk', and I determined that I would give up my job if I had another blank spell. But I was getting steadily stronger, and I did not have another attack for over two years. Lastly, I thought the reason why Ageyle called me Tommy was because I was English and had been a soldier. Prostitutes called our soldiers Tommy and American soldiers Joe. Even so, the fact that she thought my name was Tommy Grant did make me wonder.

The name Tommy held an important place in my memory.

*　　　*　　　*

I cannot remember how old I was when my mother discovered the song in a book she had bought in Chi penham. I associate the tune—I do not know why—with the long, green lawn that sloped down to the grey façade of the small William and Mary house in Wiltshire where we lived until I was seventeen. I can only remember the first line of the song:

'Now Tommy was a naughty boy, as naughty as could be.'

Then followed a list of Tommy's misdemeanours, which were considerable. He teased girls and pulled their hair; he threw things out of the window; and once, I seem to recollect, he even assaulted his father. He was a thoroughly bad type of juvenile delinquent. And he fascinated me. The recital of his misdeeds in the song was too short. I begged my mother to tell me more about him, for I was convinced he was a real person. Although my mother was unsuccessful as a novelist, she had a fertile mind, and I think she was amused by my eagerness. As a reward if I had not been tiresome all day she would come and sit by my bed after Annie, my nurse, had tucked me up, and tell me stories about Tommy.

His behaviour was flagrant. Against the direct orders of his father he had climbed up a gigantic tree and slipped, and had only been saved from death by falling into a hammock. While staying with his unfortunate parents at Worthing he had stolen a small sailing-boat and put to sea with the intention of reaching France, but a violent storm had arisen, and he would certainly have been drowned had he not been rescued by a passing destroyer. He had been caught poaching by a huge gamekeeper, who decided to hand him over to the police; Tommy had only just managed to escape in time by kicking the man sharply on the shins.

I realise now that a conflict must have arisen in my mother's mind between the moralist who felt that retribution should follow wickedness and the artist who wanted her story to be a success. But there was little hope for the moralist, because I was so devoted to Tommy that if I heard he was going to be punished I would burst into tears and sob insistently throughout the night until I was told authoritatively that the punishment had been cancelled and that Tommy was well and happy again.

Sometimes a tinge of wistfulness would seep into the

stories my mother told me. Perhaps Tommy was the kind of son that secretly she had always wanted. He was certainly very unlike me—not that I was good. I was tiresome; I did silly things like painting noughts and crosses on my bedroom wall and crying whenever the old Crossley backfired; I was always nervous and often petulant and sulky. But I was never really wicked, and I was never brave. I would never have dared to climb up a tall tree—especially if my father had told me not to. I would never have stolen a sailing-boat, nor would I have had the courage to kick a hefty game-keeper on the shins. I would certainly never have dared to attack my father, though I loathed him intensely. I was more frightened of my father than of anyone I had met, even though he had never used or threatened to use violence against me. But Tommy wasn't frightened. My mother was there to prove it. Tommy defied his father time and again, and even answered him back—instead of leaving the room in tears, as I did. I reminded myself that Tommy was at least three years older than I was—no-one of my age could have been quite so tough. But I knew that even at the age of nine he would never have dragged his feet and stammered when strangers spoke to him.

Gradually, Tommy became the embodiment of all the things I longed to be but could never be. Not only was Tommy brave and defiant: he was strong and ruthless, good at games and a crack jockey, as well as being a fearless swimmer and an intrepid mountaineer; he was insolently brash and had never felt a twinge of nervousness in all the twelve years of his life. I use the word 'embodiment' because he was so real to me that I could see him and touch him. When Annie had gone downstairs for her supper and I was all alone in my bedroom on the top floor he would come in and lie beside me and comfort me. He had curly blond hair—mine was dark and straight—starry blue eyes, a snub nose, and a wide mouth that curled up at the ends. Sometimes he looked rather like the younger son of the Martins who owned the farm down in the valley. My father had decreed that I was not to play with Harold Martin because his father drank and was dishonest—he had argued with my father about the rent of a hay-field. Tommy, of course, would have disregarded the edict; he was different.

When I came back from my first term at Lowton Preparatory School, I found that my mother's maid had left and that Annie had taken her place. Annie now had less time to play with me, and my mother was absorbed in the new novel she was writing. For the first time I wished I had brothers and sisters.

'Why don't you make friends with that nice little girl whose people have taken that cottage at the end of the drive?' Annie suggested. 'Ever so friendly they are. Hopper's the name. He runs a grocery business in Chippenham, but they've moved out here for her holidays because the Doctor said the little girl needed real country air. She's only nine. Just your age.'

I was still cross because Annie would not play draughts with me.

'I'll think about it,' I said.

Three days later I met her. She was swinging on the end of the front drive gate. My father had forbidden me to do this, explaining that, on the lever principle, weight at one end of a gate put undue strain on the hinges at the other. When the girl saw me approach she waved to me cheerfully and swung all the faster. She had dark curly hair and light blue eyes that seemed to shine with an almost defiant vitality. But her arms and legs were slender, and her lips were very pale. I decided that she was quite wiry but delicate. This re-assured me.

'You'll break the hinges,' I said.

'Why? Is it your gate?'

'No, it belongs to my father.'

'Is he the old man with grey hair who always wears a suit and goes out with a walking-stick?'

My father was then fifty-nine.

'That's him,' I said.

'My father's only thirty-five,' she said proudly.

I decided I must show some loyalty to my family.

'My mother's not much more than that,' I said.

'My mother's only thirty.'

I felt I was losing ground.

'What kind of car have your people got?' I asked.

'No kind. We've got a motor-bike and sidecar. It fair goes whizzing along. I bet our motor-bike could beat your mouldy old car any day.'

'I bet it couldn't.'

'I bet it could.'

'How much do you bet?'

'Sixpence.'

'Have you got sixpence on you?'

'No. Have you?'

'Of course I have.'

'Show me.'

I fumbled in my pocket and produced the sixpenny bit my mother had let me take off her dressing-table that morning. I held it up for her to see. Suddenly she jumped down from the gate, snatched the coin from my hand and rushed down the drive. I ran furiously after her.

'Just try and catch me!' she called over her shoulder, and swerved into the wood that flanked the drive and sloped down into the valley. And I followed her, plunging into the undergrowth, tearing my bare legs on the brambles, forcing my way through thick bushes. Fronds whipped against my face and slashed my neck, but I pressed deeper into the valley. I was close behind her and about to spring when I tripped and fell head downwards.

For an instant I was stunned. Then I felt a stabbing pain on the left side of my forehead. I put up my hand to touch the place, and it was wet. I looked with horror at the blood on my hand. I was afraid, and I wanted to cry, but I controlled myself because of the girl. There was a rustle in the bushes behind me and she appeared. She stared at me, then knelt quickly beside me.

'Got a hanky?' she asked. There was a slight tremor in her voice.

I fished in my trouser pocket and handed her a handkerchief with an acid-drop sticking to it. She popped the acid-drop into her mouth and dabbed my forehead with the clean side of the handkerchief before tying it round my head.

'You'll be all right,' she said. 'Mum can patch you up.'

'I'd better go home.'

'We live closer.'

She bent down and took my hands and pulled me up.

'What's your name?' she asked.

'Peter. What's yours?'

'Penelope. But Mum and Dad call me Penny.'

'I like Penelope.'

'I like you,' she said, and leaned forward and kissed me.

She was still holding my hands. I turned my head away so that she would not see the tears in my eyes.

'You'll be all right,' she repeated. 'Come along.'

She let go of my left hand and dragged me slowly up the hill towards their cottage.

*   *   *

When we came into their small sitting-room, Mrs. Hopper was sitting in an armchair darning socks. She was a small, plump woman with a broad, rather shiny face.

'Well, this is a surprise!' she said. 'But whatever have you done to your forehead?'

'He fell down and cut it open on a tree-stump,' Penelope said. 'Mum, can you have a look at it?'

'Of course I can. Just be a good girl and fetch me the kettle from the kitchen. Lucky it's near on the boil. And then bring me a basin. Now, young lad, sit yourself down in this chair and make yourself comfortable. We won't be long.'

While the two of them fussed around washing the little gash with a clean handkerchief dipped in warm water, tearing up an old shirt into strips to make a bandage, I lay back happily, even though I was in pain. Their evident concern made me feel brave and important. For once I had had an adventure such as Tommy might have had.

Mrs. Hopper was neatly and gently bandaging my head when Mr. Hopper came in from the back yard. He was wearing a shirt without a collar and dirty old grey flannel trousers tucked into his socks. He was a short, wiry man with sandy hair and a sharp-pointed face and red-rimmed eyes. As he stood watching us, his head cocked on one side, he reminded me of a bull-terrier.

'Hello, now what's happened?' he said. 'Been to the wars?'

'If you was to get that oil off your hands,' Mrs. Hopper said, grinning at him, 'you might get a cup of tea.'

'That's not a bad idea,' he said. 'I expect our wounded hero could do with a cup as well.'

As we sat round the table drinking tea and talking, I watched them carefully. I was convinced that the proud way they spoke of Penelope's achievements at school and the affectionate glances they gave her and her seeming love for them were all part of some monstrous deceit. I could not believe that parents and child could really be fond of each other. But when Penelope begged for chocolate biscuits and Mr. Hopper asked Mrs. Hopper to get some from her private store, and Mrs. Hopper came back with a full tin, which we finished between the four of us, I began to wonder. Surely deceit would not run to chocolate biscuits?

Penelope walked with me half the way down the drive.

'How do you feel?'

'Far better,' I lied. In fact, I felt slightly sick.

'Did you like Mum and Dad?'

'Yes, I did.'

'They liked you too.'

'How do you know?'

'The way they looked at you.'

'When can you and I meet again?'

'Tomorrow after dinner if you like.'

'After dinner?'

'Yes. I'll meet you by the white gate at three.'

'What if I'm not allowed out?'

'Why shouldn't you be?'

'I might be ill or something.'

'Don't worry. I'll be by the gate every afternoon at three till you come.'

'Thanks.'

'By the way, there's something you forgot,' she said, and held out the sixpence.

'You keep it.'

'Honest? Can I really? Thanks no end.'

I took her hand and kissed it.

'Good night, Penelope.'

'You are silly!' she said, and ran off down the drive.

*   *   *

When I reached our house it was past seven, and my mother was angry. She was angrier still when she found out who had bandaged my forehead.

'Why didn't you come straight home?'

'Their place was nearer.'

'Nonsense. They had no business to keep you. And wherever did she find that ghastly bandage?'

'It was one of Mr. Hopper's old shirts. She tore it up into strips.'

'A shirt! You don't mean to say she put that on an open cut?'

'It was perfectly clean.'

'I suppose she used some disinfectant?'

'I don't think so.'

'The woman must be criminally insane. Now, darling, we'll go straight up to my bedroom and I'll get out the medicine chest and bandage you up properly.'

That evening for the first time I dreamed that I *was*

46

Tommy. I was riding a fierce black horse when I saw the pirates advancing towards Penelope across the darkening plain. I clapped my bare legs against the sides of the horse and we galloped towards her. The pirates were only a few yards off when I leaned down and swung her up on to the saddle. As we charged away into the night I could feel her cheek pressing against mine.

The following morning I was feverish, so I was kept in bed all day. I did not see Penelope again until Monday afternoon at three o'clock.

*   *   *

It was a hot afternoon without a breath of wind. The sun beat down from a clear blue sky. The bandage round my head was damp with sweat.

I found her swinging on the end of the white gate which had now dropped at least six inches.

'You'll bust the hinges,' I said.

She laughed. 'Then I won't be able to swing any more, will I?'

'Daddy will think I did it.'

'No, he won't. I shall say to him, "I bust your gate, and you can't touch me, you silly old man." '

'He'd tell your father.'

'Dad wouldn't mind. He might keep me off chocolate biscuits for a week, though,' she added thoughtfully.

47

'What shall we do this afternoon?'

'It's too hot in the sun. Let's go somewhere in the shade.'

'Do you know the stream at the bottom of the wood?'

'A real stream?'

'Yes. I saw a frog there once. Come on, I'll show you.'

It was far hotter inside the wood than out on the drive. We sat on a bank beside the stream and played a game of throwing stones onto a boulder on the far side. I found it difficult to talk. I would think of something bright to say. For a while our conversation would flow easily, then it would splutter and stop. Penelope did not help me. She was awkward and moody.

'I don't believe there *are* any frogs down here,' she said after a long silence.

'Would you like to go home?'

'Why not? If you like we could play at dressing-up. We've got masks and all kinds of things.'

'All right.'

'I know,' she cried suddenly. 'Why don't we play at dressing-up down here?'

'We've got no things.'

'Yes, we have. I can dress up in your clothes and you can dress up in mine.'

'That would just be daft.'

'Very well. If you don't want to, let's go home.'

'No, I don't mind. Let's try.'

I walked behind one of the beech trees.

'I'll throw you across my clothes,' I said. 'And you can chuck me back yours.'

'All right.'

I peeled off my shirt and shorts and threw them down to her. A few seconds later her blue cotton dress landed at my feet, and I slipped it on and walked down to the bank. She had flattened her hair, pushing it back behind her ears. My shorts fitted her exactly. Tommy might have looked as she did when he was nine.

'You're simply wonderful,' I said.

'You look plain stupid,' she laughed.

'I bet I do,' I said, and made a pirouette and fell over backwards on purpose.

'Mind out or you'll spoil my frock. Now you pretend you're me and I'll pretend I'm you. Get it?'

But the game soon palled and silence pressed down on us again.

'I've never known it so hot,' I said after a pause.

'If only we could go swimming!'

'The nearest pool's on the road to Bath.'

'Why don't we just kneel down in the stream? We can splash water over each other. At least that would get us cool.'

I hesitated. I did not want her to see me naked.

'Come on! I'm going to, anyhow,' she said, and threw off my shirt and shorts, slipped off her vest and knickers, and stepped naked into the shallow stream.

49

'Coward!' she called out. 'Aren't you coming down?'

Her frock had begun to embarrass me. I pulled it off, kicked off my shoes, took off my pants and climbed down the bank. Even before I had reached the stream she began splashing me, scooping up the water in her hands, laughing when she saw me flinch as the ice-cold drops poured down me. I knelt down quickly and churned my arms round like a flail, showering water over her.

'Now who's the coward?' I called out, as she moved away, choking and laughing.

Suddenly, she sprang up the bank, seized her clothes and mine, and ran away with them.

'Now what will you do?' she cried.

I leaped up the bank and rushed after her. She could not run fast carrying a bundle of clothes, and I soon gained on her as she ran along the bank of the stream. When I was close behind her, she swerved towards a beech tree and flung herself down on a stretch of moss between the roots. I was so close to her that I could not stop, and fell down beside her. She tried to scramble up again but I grabbed her arm.

'You beast! Let me go!'

'Then give me back my clothes,' I said, laughing.

'I won't.'

'Oh, yes, you will,' I said, and snatched hold of her other arm. But she twisted round in my grip and flung her leg over mine. For a while we wrestled fiercely. Then, as if by mutual consent, at the very same moment, we both stopped struggling and lay without

50

moving, our bodies locked together, her cheek against mine.

*   *   *

While the rooks cawed in the branches of the beech tree high above our heads, and the bees droned round the honeysuckle by the stream, we lay together motionless, without speaking. And gradually a peace such as I had never known crept over me. I felt as if I were a ship that had been lashed by fierce winds and foaming waves but now had passed through the entrance to the harbour and was gliding across flat, calm water towards security. The taut sails could be furled and the ropes loosened.

Then at last I felt the bonds that had kept me caged up in myself melting away, and I was released from the constraint of shyness, and holding her in my arms, I poured out the fears and loneliness from my heart. I told her of my father who disliked me because I disappointed him, of my mother who loved me only when I did nothing to annoy her, of my form master at Lowton, Mr. Merrick, another old man in his fifties who loathed me; I described his sallow, hairless face and the stare of his pale green eyes that seemed to pierce through your desk and his quick sarcasm as he jingled the coins in his pocket. I told her of the night I had woken up in the dormitory to find him bending over me. When I screamed he had moved swiftly away, and the others had said it was only a dream. But I knew that he had been there because I had smelled him, and because the next morning in class he had turned his sarcasm against me so that soon he had all of them laughing at my stupidity. And as I spoke, Penelope's arms held me closer, as if the pressure of her body could drive my fears away.

The sun was slanting through the trees when we got up and dressed and with our hands linked made our way towards the drive.

'Can we meet tomorrow at the same time?' I asked.

'What are you doing in the morning?'

'Got to go into Bath to see the dentist.'

'Right. Three o'clock, then.'

'Where?'

'By the stream. But we'd better keep our place secret.'

'I won't tell anyone.'

She stopped and kissed me on the lips.

'Do you like me?'

'More than anyone,' I said truthfully.

*   *   *

The following afternoon I found her waiting for me by the stream. The feeling of security had left me. I felt nervous and embarrassed. Once again I could think of little to say, and our conversation limped along awkwardly. Presently she took my hand and drew me towards the bed of moss between the roots of the tall

52

beech and knelt down, her hands in her lap. I lay down beside her. For an instant she did not move. Then she raised her hands and began gently to unbutton my shirt.

During the next seven days of warm sunshine that followed we met every afternoon by the stream. In the morning we might play catch or touch-last on the lawn, or, if we had money, walk down to the village to buy sweets. But at three, without a word being said, we would meet under the beech tree and strip off our clothes and lie down and clasp our arms round each other as if we were two halves of one single being and could only become complete when joined together. Our happiness was so intense that for the first few minutes we never spoke, but lay quietly together listening to the rooks flapping through the tall branches, inhaling the heady stench of the wild garlic that grew thickly around us. Later we would begin to talk, sharing our secrets, discussing our problems, planning excursions we should never be allowed to make.

Penelope enjoyed life. She was devoted to her parents and basked in their affection. She was amused by the school she went to in Chippenham and excited by making new friends. And as the days passed, she was able to communicate something of her happiness to me. I no longer felt lonely. I no longer lay awake yearning for Tommy. I had a friend at last, and tomorrow I would hold her in my arms and feel her breath against my cheek.

*   *   *

53

The blow fell on Saturday morning at breakfast. I knew from the expression on my mother's face as she lifted her head to be kissed good-morning that something was wrong. My father was slitting open his letters in silence with a fruit-knife. I helped myself to porridge and cream and sat down between them.

'Darling, have you been playing with that gate at the end of the drive?' my mother asked.

'No.'

My father put down his knife and turned towards me.

'You haven't been swinging on it?'

'No.'

'At any time?'

'No.'

'Then perhaps you can explain to us why, on returning from Bath yesterday evening, we should have discovered that the hinges were broken?'

I was silent. I was afraid I was in for a cross-examination. My father was a solicitor, but I had heard my mother say he fancied himself as a barrister.

'I am asking you a question, Peter.'

'I know.'

'Then I suggest you should be good enough to answer it.'

'I didn't know the hinges were broken.'

'You have not answered my question. I am asking you if you can explain why they should have been broken.'

'No, I can't,' I mumbled.

'You can't or you won't?'

'Evelyn . . .' my mother began.

'Kindly allow me to handle this matter as I think fit. You can't or you won't?'

'I can't.'

'You haven't ever swung on the gate?'

'No.'

'Is that true? Think carefully.'

'Not since you told me not to.'

'And you know of no-one else who has been tampering with the gate?'

'No.'

'That girl you play with lives in the cottage opposite, doesn't she?'

'Yes.'

'You have never seen her swinging on the gate?'

'No.'

'That is strange—because two of our servants have. And since you tell us that you have not injured the gate, I can only presume that she is responsible. I shall therefore be forced to visit her father and demand compensation for the price of two new hinges and the cost of replacing them.'

There was silence. My father took up his knife and began slitting open another envelope.

'I was wrong,' I said. 'I did swing on the gate.'

'So you lied to us?'

'No. I just forgot.'

'You just forgot?'

'I only did it once after you told me not to.'

55

'And when was that?'

'Yesterday evening.'

'So you did break the hinges?'

'Evelyn, please . . .' my mother said quietly.

'I must insist on being allowed to deal with this myself. I'm afraid, my dear Mary, that you fail to appreciate the seriousness of the matter. Property has been damaged. It is our duty to find out who damaged it. Now, Peter, did you break those hinges?'

'They weren't broken when I left.'

'I suppose they snapped by chance a few minutes later?'

'I don't know,' I mumbled.

My father saw that I was about to break down, and he had a fastidious dislike of scenes.

'Very well,' he said. 'You have lied to us and you admit disobeying me. You can go up to your room and remain there until supper-time.'

'But, Evelyn, it's such a lovely day,' my mother protested.

My father turned away from her impatiently.

'I presume you have a holiday task,' he said.

'Yes.'

'What is it?'

'*Pilgrim's Progress.*'

'Have you started it?'

'Yes. Well, not really.'

'What do you mean—"not really"?'

'I've looked through it.'

'Well now, I suggest you should start to read through

it. I shall examine you myself this evening. Now you may go.'

As I stumbled from the room I heard him say to my mother:

'My dear Mary, merely because he's an only child there's no reason . . .'

Then the door closed and I walked wretchedly up the oak staircase to the top floor.

I paced nervously up and down my room until Annie came in to console me. She had heard of my disgrace through the curious grapevine that seemed to run between the dining-room, the nursery and the servants' hall. Perhaps Jenkins the parlourmaid had overheard from the scullery.

I could not bear to think of Penelope waiting for me by the stream. When Annie produced two pencils and a block of paper and suggested we play noughts and crosses, I knew what I must do. I took the pad and laboriously wrote out in my best script:

'I cannot be there today. See you tomorrow. Peter.'

Annie was afraid to deliver it. But after half an hour of cajoling she agreed to give it to the errand-boy from the village who usually called about eleven o'clock. So I wrote out the full address on an envelope.

*   *   *

When I heard my father's footsteps on the stairs that evening I pushed my Meccano set under the bed and took up the book. I had reached page thirty-five. Christian had just met Mr. Worldly Wiseman. I stood up when my father came into the room. His face was white, which meant that he was angry. He walked slowly across to the chimney-piece.

'Sit down, Peter,' he said. 'I shall not examine you on *Pilgrim's Progress* this evening, because I have something more important to say to you. As you may know, your mother and I have a certain position to maintain in the village, and we must therefore be careful with whom we consort. This evening I had occasion to call on Mr. Hopper in order to ask him in all civility to stop his daughter from damaging my gate. I found him offensive and insolent, and Mrs. Hopper was no better. Evidently they are a thoroughly common family. You will appreciate therefore that I must ask you never to see that daughter of theirs again.'

*   *   *

By the following morning I had made my plans. I had decided that I could risk meeting Penelope for an hour each day by the stream. I relied on Annie to provide some excuse if my absence from the garden was noticed by my father; I knew my mother would not betray me, even though she did so little to help.

It was a hot, airless day. The sun was burning down from a white sky when I left the house at half-past two. My father was lying on the lawn by the mulberry tree at the end of the slope. I thought he was asleep, but as I crept up the drive he opened his eyes and called me.

'Where are you going?'

'Just up to the top. It's cooler up there.'

'I'd rather you played in the garden this afternoon. I shall call you in twenty minutes' time to make sure you're still about.'

He sighed and closed his eyes again. Twenty minutes would not allow me time to get to the stream and back. I must send another message. But Annie had gone into Bath with my mother, and there was no-one else I could trust. I was wandering aimlessly across the lawn when I noticed the roller that Anstey, our gardener, swore was the heaviest type that one man could push alone. It was poised on the very edge of the slope so that there seemed no reason why it did not run down the incline and crash against the mulberry tree. I approached it cautiously. Then I saw that it was prevented from rolling down the slope by two square wooden blocks jammed in at either end of the iron roller so that a sharp blow would dislodge them.

The heat was intense, almost suffocating—as if the force of the sun had drawn away all the air from the valley. I felt suddenly weak. I lay down at the top of the lawn and closed my eyes. Though my limbs felt heavy, my head was oddly light. Fantastic images and scenes flashed across my mind. Penelope was riding the black horse across a field of red earth; her cheeks and the horse's flanks were bespattered with red mud. I was gliding along beside her, my feet scarcely touching the ground, when a gob of mud splashed against my forehead. I put up my hand to brush it away, and my fingers became sticky with blood. Then the dining-room swung into my mind. My porridge was in a bowl on the table in front of me; if I began to eat they would see my red hands. I wiped them furtively on my napkin, but my father had noticed.

'Show me your hands,' he said. 'Show me your hands.'

I did not move. He leaned across and snatched the napkin away from me.

'Peter! Peter!'

It must be my father calling to make certain I was still in the garden.

'I'm here,' I called out. 'On the lawn.'

I could feel the heat exuding from the turf. I felt wonderfully drowsy. When I closed my eyes again I was in the dormitory at Lowton—and alone. Perhaps I had been sent to bed early, for a faint glimmer of remaining daylight filtered in through the rep curtains. I looked up. Mr. Merrick was standing by my bed, staring down at me with his pale green eyes. I tried to scream but no sound came. Then he bent down, and slowly his cold, white, scaly fingers began to fumble near my throat. Suddenly I felt a surge of power flow through me like an electric charge. I was no longer afraid and trembling; I was strong and brave. I flung away his hands from my body and sprang out of bed and struck my fist into his face. He fell in a crumpled

60

heap. I charged down the corridor, shouting wildly, exulting in my new-found vigour. Then the green baize doors at the far end of the passage opened and my father appeared. His face was very white and his hands were shaking as they did when he was near to losing control.

'Go back to Mr. Merrick,' he said. 'He's calling for you. He wants you.'

'I won't.'

'Do you dare to disobey me?'

I tried to swerve past him, but he caught my arm in a hard grip and with his other hand he slapped my face. As I felt the tears sting my lids I was filled with a passionate anger. Rage swept over me like a great tide, swirling round my head, coursing through my veins. I leaped at him as he stood by the open window and forced him back, step by step. Then with a last convulsive shudder of strength I thrust him away, and he fell backwards screaming. I ran to the window and looked down. He lay in the courtyard with his arms and legs spread out as if he were embracing the flagstones. Blood was oozing from his head.

I awoke feeling sick and dizzy. The warm turf was no longer friendly. There was menace in the hot, sweet scent of the grass. I jumped up, ran into the house, rushed up the stairs into my room and lay sweating on my bed.

I was asleep when Annie found me.

'So that's where you've been all afternoon! We've been looking for you everywhere.'

61

'I must have dozed off,' I said. I still felt drugged with sleep.

'With this terrible heat I'm not surprised. Now listen, ducky, there's been a nasty accident, but you're not to get upset. Your Daddy will be back again with us inside a month, I shouldn't be surprised.'

'Daddy?'

'You know that great big roller what Anstey has for the lawn? Well, he'd left it on the top of the lawn with them blocks under it, but somehow it got started and rolled down. It's crushed one of your father's legs and broken the other. They've taken him off in an ambulance.'

I was filled with a delirious joy, for I realised that I would now be able to see Penelope the very next day, but I knew that sorrow was expected of me. I tried to find the right words.

'Is he in hospital now?'

'Should be. Your Mummy's gone with him. We got back from Bath just after it had happened. I'm surprised you didn't hear all the commotion.'

I thought about my dream.

'Did it hurt his head?'

'It ran over his legs, I'm telling you. The rest of him is unharmed, heaven be praised.'

'Did he scream?'

'I've never known a man so brave as he was when they were carrying him into the ambulance. I only hope you grow up to be like him.'

'What time did it happen?'

'Four o'clock.'

'How did the roller start moving?'

Annie paused for a moment before answering.

'No-one quite knows. But don't you fuss your little head about it. You were up here and asleep, and that's that.'

*   *   *

Later that evening my mother came and sat beside my bed.

'Daddy's going to be all right,' she said. 'They've given him morphine, so he's no longer in pain.'

'I'm glad.'

'Peter, you didn't see anyone playing about near that roller, did you?'

'No.'

'Your father says you were on the lawn earlier on in the afternoon.'

'Yes, I was.'

'You didn't pull those wooden blocks away, did you?'

'No.'

'I mean, we know that you mightn't have realised how dangerous it was.'

'I never touched them.'

'And about three you came up here to lie down?'

'Yes, Mummy.'

'Weren't you feeling very well?'

63

'I felt dizzy and my head ached.'

'Do you think you've got a temperature?'

'No. Annie took it just now.'

'Peter, can you think of anyone who might have pulled those blocks of wood away?'

'No, Mummy, I can't.'

'You're certain?'

'Dead certain.'

'You don't think . . .' she began. Then she stopped and kissed me goodnight and left the room.

*   *   *

When I was lying with Penelope in our secret meeting-place the following afternoon, she noticed that I was unusually glum.

'You don't mind that he's been taken off to hospital, do you?' she asked.

'No.'

'Then what's wrong?'

'Penelope, you didn't kick those blocks away, did you?'

She gazed up at me steadily with large blue eyes.

'No, I didn't. But if I'd known he was trying to stop us meeting I might have done.'

'Who can have done it?'

'Perhaps it was Anstey. I've heard him cursing your father like one o'clock.'

'Do you think he'd have dared?'

64

'Your Dad was asleep, wasn't he?'
'Penelope, do you really love me?'
'Yes, I do.'
'Why?'
'Because you smell nice.'
'Will you miss me?'
'Don't talk of that. We've whole weeks ahead of us. Move your arm a little. There. That's better.'

     *   *   *

Every day of August—even when it rained—I met Penelope under the beech by the stream, and gradually I grew stronger and happier, though I dreaded the moment when we should have to say goodbye. But Penelope promised that she would write every week and that she would persuade her parents to take the cottage again for the Christmas holidays, and I believed it as her hot tears fell onto my cheek our last afternoon together; for I believed that we were so close together, so much part of one single being, that neither time nor space could divide us.

But she never answered my letters, and soon I gave up writing to her. And when I returned home at Christmas I learned that Mr. Hopper had bought a grocery business in the Midlands and all three of them had moved to Leeds. I never saw her again. But by the time the next summer holidays began, hot, groping hands had initiated me into the mysteries of sex, the seal of my virginity had been broken, and I could never have lain with her in innocence again.

*   *   *

I have lit the Aladdin lamps, and I have just had my third whisky.

As I drank I thought how fortunate I was to have known a love as direct and uncomplicated as that between Penelope and me. Yet I was also unfortunate, for it was inevitable that I should never find it again, though I never gave up the search for it, and I suppose I never shall. As the terms at Lowton passed by, the weeks I had spent with Penelope became unreal. I could still see the bed of moss between the grey roots of the tree, and her delicate, ivory-coloured body lying half curled up in sleep. But the picture that swung into my mind was quite remote, as if it were a slide from a magic-lantern show I had seen many years previously. The reality was Tommy, who was daily in my mind and often, I fancied, standing close to me, comforting and protecting me. When I lay trembling in bed it was Tommy whose hands were there to soothe my twitching limbs. For all his wickedness in dealing with other people, so far as I was concerned Tommy had become a guardian angel. His presence did not leave me until I was sixteen and the worst horrors of life at school were behind me. Even after he had gone I did not believe he was dead; I felt he was waiting in some limbo, ready to spring back into my life should I need him.

I therefore realised that it was easily possible that in my black-out I should give the name of Tommy to Ageyle. But I knew that I did not 'change' into Tommy as Dr. Jekyll 'changed' into Mr. Hyde because, I repeat, I had asked several friends who had been in the same room with me, as Edward was, when I blacked out, if they had noticed any marked change, and they had not observed any difference in me. No-one as yet had *even known* when I had lost consciousness. There could be no question of any complete 'change of personality'. Or so I thought until the episode in Tangier in October, two years later.

*   *   *

I first noticed him as I sat drinking coffee laced with Spanish brandy at the Café Central in the Zoco Chico —the tiny square in the heart of the medina in Tangier. I had not walked down into town for several weeks because I had been working hard on the last chapters of my travel book. But this evening I had reason to celebrate, for the publishers to whom I had sent the first half of the book had written me an enthusiastic letter accepting it.

I felt elated yet serene, and I had not had a black-out for well over two years.

I noticed him for two reasons: first, because with his

curly fair hair and snub nose and wide mouth he looked rather like Tommy might have at twenty-five; secondly, because I knew something about his companion, a slim Spaniard of about fifty with whom he was talking intently as they sat drinking beer at the Café Fuentes opposite. Julian Tuke, who worked in a section of the British Legation and who was my 'contact' in Tangier, had pointed out the Spaniard to me the second evening we had spent together. He was a Republican refugee who was suspected of being a Communist agent. He was known to be in communication with the Arab nationalist leaders in the Spanish and French zones of Morocco. The International zone of Tangier, with its free exchange and clutter of banks, was the centre from which the Communists distributed money to sources most likely to embarrass the Western powers.

I was wondering what the young Englishman—I was almost certain he was English, with his stained leather jerkin and patched grey flannel trousers—could be discussing so eagerly with his companion, when Julian Tuke, for whom I had been waiting, sat down at my table. Julian was a slender man and so tall that he had developed an apologetic stoop. His bony forehead, receding hair and rimless glasses, combined with his love of using French words which he dragged ruthlessly into his conversation, reminded me of a lecturer from the British Council, but he was supposed to be one of the most efficient intelligence officers in North Africa, probably because he had an alert brain and was devoid of compassion. He ordered a coffee and a Fundador and then smiled at me maliciously.

'I see that you've spotted our friend opposite,' he said.

I was mildly annoyed, for I had been training myself to watch people discreetly.

'Who's the young man with him?' I asked.

'Name on passport—James Hugh Burge. But known around the harbour as Jim. Age—twenty-seven. Born in London. Served in the Navy during the war as a mechanician in small ships, mostly motor torpedo vessels and the like. Single. Came out here in 'forty-six as chief engineer on a converted M.T.V. that began smuggling cigarettes between here and Naples *comme d'habitude*. As you know, there's nothing illegal about taking cigarettes out of this harbour, so we can't stop them provided their papers are in order. And for a time their trips were successful. Then an Italian patrol nearly caught them off Ischia and they had to dump their cargo into the sea. Came back almost broke. Then Jim had a row with the Captain, and he's been drifting about ever since—until last week. And that's when we became really interested in him.'

'Why?'

'He's signed on as second engineer on board a five-hundred-ton diesel yacht that's been converted to carry cargo. The yacht's French-built. Her name is the *Salomé*, and she's registered in Panama.'

'What's interesting about that?'

'Nothing. But at present the nominal registered owner is Antonio Silva, our Spanish friend opposite.'

'Do you think . . .'

Julian raised a large, bony hand to silence me.

'Did you know you were going to be asked to work in this area for another year?' he asked.

'I hoped I would be.'

'Well, so far as we're concerned it's all taped.'

'Who gives me my instructions?'

Julian looked down at his glass of brandy and smiled almost bashfully.

'I do,' he said.

'When do I start?'

'Tonight, if you like.'

'What can I do?'

'Find out what cargo the *Salomé* is really carrying. It's more than cigarettes this time, I'm certain.'

'Such as?'

'Chemicals and perhaps people.'

'Where's the ship going to?'

'Nominally—to Hamburg. In reality—to some port on the wrong side of the Iron Curtain.'

'Why should it carry passengers?'

'There are various people wanted by the French and Spanish police who could be very useful in Moscow, *tu sais.*'

Julian bent over his brandy like a stork and sipped cautiously. Then he drew out a white silk handkerchief from his sleeve and wiped his lips.

'Unless I'm very much wrong,' he continued, 'I don't think Jim's any more of a Communist than you are, *mon cher.* I believe he's in this game for the money and the excitement of it. He doesn't quite know how dangerous it is. If you were to persuade him to come clean you'd be doing him a good turn as well as us.'

'Persuade?'

'I should play it on two levels if I were you—patriotism and self-interest. Plug that he's helping a potential enemy. His type are usually delightfully patriotic *au fond*. Then you can mention *en passant* that a hundred pounds might tide him over the next few weeks or so.

'Anything else?'

Julian smiled and blinked shyly through his spectacles.

'One advantage of working in this place is that everyone thinks everyone else is a spy, so one can really afford to relax security. For instance, I can afford to be seen talking to you. But never forget this,' he said softly. 'Should there be any trouble we'll disown you flat.'

He handed the waiter some peseta notes and stood up carefully, as if he were afraid that any sudden movement might fracture a limb.

'No hurry,' he said, with a polite nod of his head. 'Any time this week. *A bientôt!*'

And he strolled slowly away.

*　　　*　　　*

71

Without appearing obvious, I tried to watch Jim and his companion as they sat at their little table outside the café, a few yards across the narrow street that led down from the Zoco Grande to the harbour. Cars were not allowed to drive through the Zoco Chico, but my vision was filtered by the crowds swarming past— Moors striding by like proud monks in their hoods and long cloaks, Berber women with white robes and broad mushroom hats, hordes of pallid children and beggars, quickly-moving businessmen in European clothes, wizened-faced shoe-blacks, veiled Moslem women teetering on spiked high-heeled shoes. But I could see that it was the Spaniard who was talking now, and that Jim had started drinking brandy. He was leaning over the table, scowling with the effort to understand what was being said to him.

I decided that since there was no hurry and as I had been seen talking to Julian, who was known to work in the British Legation, I would not approach Jim that night; I would continue my private celebration. I did not feel like going to any of the smart bars; I would not go to Dean's, for all his wit and charm, nor would I sit in the spacious courtyard of the hotel Minzah and drink beer at seven shillings a glass. I finished my brandy and wandered along one of the narrow alley-ways that led from the Zoco Chico.

I wandered for an hour or so, past little stalls and small hotels with odd names such as 'Satan' or 'Delirium', past the hovels of the brothel quarter, with a raddled young girl staring from each door; on I walked, disregarding the hands of pimps clutching eagerly at my sleeve and the whining voice repeating like a dirge the familiar words: 'Hey, Johnnie! You want hotel? You come with me. Me your freng. You my freng. Mister, Mister! You wan like I no spick wid you? Mister, Mister!'—past dusty passage-ways, past ragged, dark men looking sullenly at any foreigner, past skinny boys with hollow eyes huddled in unlit corners.

Now and then I would stop at one of the smaller Spanish bars, where the wine ran from huge wooden vats that stretched up to the whitewashed, vaulted ceiling and the air was heavy with the smell of garlic, and drink glass after glass of light, dry sherry, and then move out into lurid alley-ways littered with refuse and excrement and walk until I felt like drinking again. And as I walked through these narrow streets—no more than a slit between the houses—I believed I could understand why the Arabs felt that life was timeless and man must forever suffer his sores, his lice and disease, and his loneliness. For they knew that man has always been acquainted with pain: it has taken its turn in his consciousness together with hunger and lust, inevitably, like sunset. Man must suffer. That, say the Arabs, is in the order of things. So the tiny child must crouch by the loom in the shop-corner, and the deformed girl must crawl on the stumps of her knees to buy bread, and flies must crawl round the sticky red sores on the beggar's forehead, and the force of life must flow and throb relentlessly through the black arteries of the medina.

73

It was one o'clock by the time I reached the bar that overlooked the harbour and stayed open all night. Leaning against the sea-wall outside were some of the older male prostitutes, two or three pimps and a few toughs from the harbour-front. The door was open, and I could hear the voice of the old fat Spanish woman, harshly strident but wonderfully true, as she sang the flamenco songs she knew so well. I walked inside. The place was crowded. To the left as I came in was a group of Spaniards, absorbed in listening to the flamenco singer, clapping hands to the rhythm, joining in the choruses, oblivious to all outside their circle. In the centre, sitting at small tables, were a few businessmen with their hangers-on, smoking feverishly, as if their success depended on it, a few merchant-seamen with some local European prostitutes, and a couple of male American tourists, nervously fingering their Leicas and exchanging shy glances as if to congratulate each other on being brave enough to enter the place. Opposite me was the bar—a large slab of marble with a mirror running the full length of the wall behind it. Written in white paint on the mirror was 'Hay Pajaritos Fritos'—fried sparrows, one of the place's specialities. As I looked around vaguely, through the crowd, at the dirty green walls, the damp sawdust on the floor, the garish advertisements for American drinks, the hideous fluorescent lighting, I noticed Jim in the far corner. He was leaning on his elbows, scowling at the barman who was chalking up another drink to his account which was scribbled in pesetas on the counter. I could see him perfectly in the mirror. A strand of hair had fallen over his forehead and touched his thick eyebrows, which I noticed were of a darker colour. His surprisingly light blue eyes were dilated and gleaming. I was wondering if he had drunk as much as I had when a tall, thick-set man with a square, fleshy face appeared in the doorway. He wore a heavy fisherman's sweater and yellow corduroy trousers. A thick gold chain hung from his right wrist, the gold strap of his watch glittered on the other. He stood for a moment staring at the men leaning against the bar. Then he saw Jim. Immediately he turned round and walked out. By moving my position slightly I could see the lamplit street outside reflected in the mirror, and I saw the man beckon to one of the group sprawling on the wall, a young Berber with a lean, effeminate face. For a moment they whispered together. Then he handed the boy some notes, the boy nodded, and the man returned again to the bar. But this time he walked straight up to Jim and tapped him on the shoulder. Jim turned round slowly. I edged my way closer to them.

'I've been looking for you,' the man said. His English voice was deep, yet his accent was refined, almost prissy.

'You didn't have to look far,' Jim said. 'I've been here nearly every night.'

'No, I didn't have to look far.'

'So what, then?' Jim asked impatiently. His voice was hoarse, like that of a young boy.

'So I saw you this evening. I saw you talking to a cheap Commie.'

'I'll talk with who I like. You're not my boss any more.'

'No?'

'I signed off. Remember?'

'And now you've signed on with the Commies. I hope they don't ask too much of you.'

'Meaning just what?'

'You weren't too particular in London. Remember?'

The flush rose from Jim's neck and spread over his face.

'You're asking for it,' he said hoarsely.

The man looked down at Jim's fists and smiled.

'Not in here,' he said gently.

'Then come outside.'

'If that's what you want,' the man said, and walked slowly out of the bar.

Jim was following him when I moved across and caught hold of his arm. He turned furiously.

'Leave me alone.'

'I've got to speak to you.'

'What the hell do you want? Let go of me.'

'Just two minutes ago I saw that man who's just left give money to a boy from the gang outside. If you follow him you'll get beaten up.'

Jim stared at me, searching my face with his red-rimmed eyes.

'You're lying.'

I dropped my hand from his arm.

76

'Why should I lie? I don't even know you.'

'Why should you care if I get beaten up? Just who are you, anyway?'

'If you give me a chance,' I said, 'I can answer both your questions.'

At that moment the man came back and stood in the doorway.

'Are you coming?' he called out. 'Or are you just chicken?'

'I'll answer both your questions,' I said to Jim quietly. 'And I might even be able to help you.'

Jim glanced at me, then turned back to the man.

'Get out,' he said to him. 'Find some other matelot to muck about. I just don't want to know.'

The man hesitated, then he swung round and disappeared.

'Now,' I said. 'What about a drink?'

*   *   *

An hour later I had heard a rough outline of Jim's life-story. There was little unusual about it—childhood in the slums of Bethnal Green, quarrelling parents, an elder brother who ran away to sea, his parents' divorce, joining a street gang, two years of an Approved School, and then the war. Life in the Navy, demobilisation and a violent disillusionment, 'on the bat' in London for a year, the tempting offer of a job as chief engineer on an M.T.V. with a share in the profit if the cigarettes

77

were delivered successfully, the trip when they were nearly caught, the break-up of the crew. I had heard similar stories before. But two things struck me: though he was very frank in talking about events up to the end of the war, he was reticent about his relationship with the hefty man with the affected voice, who evidently had been the skipper, if not the owner, of the boat, and he refused to say anything about his present job.

The door of the bar had been shut and the air was thick with smoke.

Though he was only mildly drunk, Jim's forehead was shining with sweat.

'What about going out for a breather?' he asked.

'Careful of the gang outside.'

'They won't attack if we're together.'

We walked cautiously along the ramparts that led up to the Zoco Chico. The cafés were deserted.

'What about coming up to my place?' Jim suggested suddenly. 'My friend who owns it is away in Gib, so we'll be alone, and I've got a case of beer.'

'Fine.'

We walked in silence up the Rue de Siaghines and through the Zoco Grande. The empty stalls gleamed in the cold moonlight. As we were crossing the Place de France Jim turned and looked at me.

'What did you mean about being able to help me?' he asked.

'I'll tell you one day.'

'Why not tonight—or what's left of it?'

'Perhaps.'

We turned up a side street leading off the Boulevard Pasteur and stopped in front of an antique shop. Through the iron grille of the shutters I could see an array of baroque cherubs reclining on red velvet and surrounded by a collection of musical boxes. A discreet shop sign above the grille read: J. MOLENAR, ANTI-QUAIRE.

Jim opened a door set in the grille with a latch-key and switched on a light, and we walked inside. Fans and shawls, a collection of aquatints, pieces of Moroccan pottery, Saracen helmets and swords, all covered with dust, were littered around a set of Louis Seize gilt chairs. Through an alcove at the far end of the room was a Jacobean four-poster bed covered with a blue silk quilt.

'I'm allowed to sleep here when the boss is away,' Jim said. 'What about some beer?'

We sat on gilt chairs drinking Pilsener out of the bottle. I was trying to think of something to say to break the silence when Jim got up abruptly.

'You must hear my favourite piece,' he said, and strode across to the largest of the musical-boxes, opened the ebony lid, wound the handle, set the indicator, pressed down a lever at the side, and with a faint rustle the tinkling music began.

One or two of the notes were missing and at first I did not recognise the tune. Then I looked towards Jim in surprise.

'Do you know it?' he asked.

'Yes.'

'What's it called? The name's rubbed away on the list.'

'Jesu, joy of man's desiring.'

Immediately his face brightened.

'That's right,' he said. 'That's just what the old girl told me it was.'

He looked at me gratefully, as if somehow I had confirmed that a friend had not betrayed him in an important matter.

'Who's the old girl?'

Once again the cautious, almost hostile, look came back into his violet eyes.

'Just a friend I made when I was hard up. She owns this place.'

'Do you like classical music?' I asked, to change the conversation.

'Don't know much about it. But I like this. Listen. You can hear it's got something.'

Above the whirring of the clockwork motor we listened to the metallic notes as they fell tinkling into the dusty room. And as I listened the shutter fell down over my mind.

*　　　*　　　*

I remembered nothing until I woke up lying fully dressed on my bed in the room I had taken in a villa perched on the top of the Marshan. I gazed around wretchedly at the water-colours of Paris on the wall and the rickety French furniture. The sun was already warming the room. I looked at my watch. It was noon. I felt very thirsty and slightly sick. I drank the glass of water by my bed. Then I went through the routine I had not needed to use for over two years. I examined my wallet. No money seemed to be missing. I looked at my little engagement book. There were no fresh entries. I walked over to the mirror and examined my face and my clothes for any clue as to where I had been after leaving the antique shop. There were no lipstick marks on my face or shirt, nor was there any lingering trace of scent.

And yet, as I stared at my pale face in the mirror, I realised that it was not quite accurate to suppose that I remembered nothing from the moment when I had been listening to the musical box. This time my black-out had not been complete, for vague recollections of the evening now came filtering through. I could see Jim pacing up and down the room, his hair falling over his forehead, his eyes shining, the words pouring out in a rush, as if a lock-gate in his mind had been suddenly opened. And, as I gazed in the speckled mirror, stray phrases floated back into my mind. 'Jesus Christ was a Commie, wasn't he?' I could hear the hoarse voice and see the anxious yet defiant look in his eyes. 'If he was alive he'd see the form. He'd see that the bosses were no better than robbers. He'd see that the whole system can only work if there's a class war between those who buy labour as cheap as possible and those who sell it as dear as possible. And he'd know there was only one way to end class warfare.'

The trite argument revolted me, yet my incoherent memories of the hours before dawn had left me with feelings amounting almost to affection for Jim. Perhaps it was his shy charm combined with his sincerity. I decided that when I got the chance I would try to reason with him. But the awkward fact remained. For the time being he was—to use Julian's phrase—'playing for the wrong team'. And he might be dangerous.

I was going through my pockets when I found a sheet of notepaper, neatly folded. I opened it and stared at the paper heading: J. MOLENAR, ANTIQUAIRE, with the address of the street off the Boulevard Pasteur beneath it. But it was not the address that made my mouth feel suddenly dry; it was the spidery writing scrawled beneath, the letters jerking up and down erratically as if someone had been clutching at the writer's hand, struggling to prevent his pen touching the paper—crabbed, shaky writing that for all its wild stabs and quavering lines was familiar to me, for it was my own.

The letters were so ill-formed that at first I could not make out the words, but I was almost certain that the first line was a name and the second an address. I brewed myself a cup of coffee and then looked at the sheet of paper again. This time I could read the name and address clearly: Mustapha Ben Salah—7, Calle Los Fuegos.

I lit a cigarette and walked out onto the terrace. Calle

Los Fuegos was one of the dark alleys I had walked through the previous night. Mustapha Ben Salah was the leader of the extremist Arab nationalist party with its underground headquarters somewhere in the medina of Fez. He was wanted for the murder of a senior French official in Rabat. He had been in hiding for six months. Then I remembered that Julian had said that the *Salomé* might carry chemicals or people. I already knew where Jim's allegiance lay. There was only one possible explanation for the name and address. During my black-out I must have persuaded him to tell me the truth about the ship. I went back into the room, finished my coffee, shaved quickly, and took a taxi down to Julian's office.

*   *   *

I found him sipping mint tea and reading the *Journal de Maroc*.

'I hear you met our young friend last night,' he said without looking up.

'Yes, I did.'

He marked a passage in the paper with a blue pencil and tossed it into his 'out' tray.

'Learn anything, *mon cher*?'

'I think so.'

Julian looked up at me for the first time.

'You're curiously reticent,' he said. 'You must *know* whether you found things out or not. After all, you were with him until eight this morning.'

I felt suddenly cold.

'I know what it is,' Julian continued. 'Your tender yet illogical conscience is disturbed at the prospect of betraying poor Jim's confidence. But you needn't worry.'

'Why not?'

'There are a dozen members of that crew.'

'He was seen talking to me, and I'd been seen with you.'

'We can protect Jim.'

'How?'

'Let me ask you a question back. How do you think I know that you left the antique shop at eight this morning? *Tu comprends?*'

'You're certain?'

Julian dropped his blue pencil onto the blotter.

'Perfectly,' he said. 'And now perhaps we can forget your noble sentiments and get down to our job. What have you got from last night?'

I had already invented an explanation of how I discovered the name and address.

'He was drunk,' I said. 'It was hot in the shop. He took off his jacket. When he went into the lavatory to be sick I had time to go through his wallet. I found a name and address written in pencil on a slip of paper. But it wasn't his writing.'

'How do you know?'

'Because I got him to write down my address on the Marshan later.'

'Can I see the slip of paper?'

84

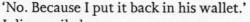

'No. Because I put it back in his wallet.'

Julian smiled.

'*Le bon élève*,' he said. 'And what was the name and what was the address?'

'Mustapha Ben Salah. 7, Calle Los Fuegos.'

Julian was silent for a moment. Then he said:

'You're sure?'

'Perfectly.'

He got up and walked across to the window.

'Mustapha could be very valuable. He may be the entire *raison d'être* of the trip. You've done well.'

'What can we do about Jim?'

'Give me twenty-four hours to work that one out. In the meantime I can at least see to it that he's safe.'

'I'd like to help him.'

Julian gave me a curious look.

'We'll do our best,' he said, and opened the door for me.

*   *   *

That night I stayed up on the Marshan working on my travel book. I knew that Julian would get in touch with me if he wanted to. There was no telephone in my room, but he had arranged with Madame Badin, who owned the villa, to have me fetched if he telephoned her private number. Madame Badin was a widow of sixty with a hook nose and frizzy grey hair. She lived alone in the main rooms of the villa, looked after by a bad-tempered, bearded Moor of about the same age. Legend said they had once been lovers; gossip suggested they still were.

The following morning at nine o'clock I was shaving when I saw the Moor shuffling across the courtyard in his worn slippers. I went to the door.

'*Teléfono!*' he grunted and shuffled crossly away again. I wiped my face and hurried after him. As usual Madame Badin was in her purple woollen dressing-gown with her hair clamped into curlers.

'It is your friend Mr. Tuke,' she said.

'Thanks.'

'*Le voilà,*' she said into the receiver, and handed me the 'phone.

'Is that you, Peter?'

For the first time since I had known him Julian sounded worried.

'Can you come down to the office right away?'

'Why? What's wrong? What's happened?'

But even as I asked I had a ghastly feeling that I knew what it was.

'I'd rather tell you down here.'

'Can't you tell me now?'

Julian hesitated. His training made him wary of discussing even the most banal matters over an open line.

'You know I'd appointed a guardian for our young friend,' he said after a pause. 'Well, he must have noticed—because at one o'clock this morning he gave him the slip. Do you get me?'

'Yes.'

'At six o'clock this morning they found our friend on a wharf quite near his ship. He'd been beaten up.'

'Badly?'

'Yes.'

'He's alive?'

'Yes.'

'Will he be all right?'

There was silence. When Julian spoke, his voice was expressionless. He might have been telling me that it was three minutes past nine.

'The doctors we've had in don't think so,' he said.

'Where is he?'

'In a nursing home. It's easier to guard than a hospital. I've slipped up once, I'm not slipping up again.'

'Can I see him?'

'That depends on the doctors. But I've told them I think it's highly important that you do see him.'

'So I can find out more from him?'

'Yes. After all he's got nothing to lose now. I should tell you that the address was perfectly correct. We ran our quarry to ground last night. What's more our young friend was in with them up to the neck, poor devil. We've had proof of it now. And you won't be surprised to hear that the ship's not sailing.'

'Is your car outside the office?'

'Yes.'

'Will you give your driver the address of the nursing-home and send him up to collect me?'

'I want to see you first.'

'I'm going to the nursing-home first. I'll see you later.'

'So that's how it is?'

'Yes.'

'*Souviens-toi . . .*'

'I haven't yet accepted. I don't have to take orders from you. Now will you please send that car?'

There was a pause. Then Julian said:

'Very well. But take your passport with you.'

And I put down the receiver.

*   *   *

While I was driven down into town I prayed that by some miracle Jim would recover, and I prayed—selfishly and stupidly—that it had been his former skipper who had been responsible for the assault.

The nursing-home was in a street above the Hotel Valentina. It was run by a plump and efficient-looking French woman who spoke almost perfect English.

'You are Mr. Grant?'

'Yes.'

'Please can you show me some identification? I am sorry to ask. But those are my instructions. I do not like this business,' she said with a jerk of her head towards the corridor. 'But what can I do?'

As I handed her my passport I saw two police officers standing in front of the door at the far end. She looked quickly at the photograph and then led me into a small waiting-room.

'I do not know if you can see him yet,' she said. 'He is very ill, I am afraid. But if you will sit down I will go and ask the Sister who is looking after him.'

I was trying to concentrate on the current number of the *Tangier Gazette* when the Sister came in. Despite the crisp starch of her cap and collar I recognised her wrinkled face immediately. Her name was Dorothy Gales. She was the widow of an English doctor who had practised in Tangier quite successfully, and had died ten years previously, leaving her a pleasant villa and a small income. She was childless, her relations bored her, and she loved her little garden and her friends in Morocco. There was no reason for her to return to England, so she had stayed on. But she was a trained nurse, and—partly to give her something to do outside her garden and the local bridge parties, partly because the value of her investments had fallen—she occasionally took nursing jobs if they interested her or she felt she was really needed. It was clever of Julian to have got hold of her, for she was efficient and reliable.

'I was expecting you,' she said. 'But there's no point in you seeing him yet, poor boy. He's still delirious.'

'Is there any . . . ?'

'No. None, I'm afraid. The specialist has just left. There's nothing more we can do. They must have used iron bars or something. I've never seen such a mess as they made of his head. And he looks so pathetically young.'

'How long do you think he'll live?'

'It's hard to say—but six hours at the most.'

'Has he been conscious at all since he came in? Has he said anything?'

She turned her raddled face towards me and stared at me with worn grey eyes.

'Is that all that you and Julian care about?'

'No,' I said. 'It's not all.'

'I wonder.'

'Please tell me. Has he said anything? Has he asked for anyone?'

'He mutters a few words, that's all.'

'But nothing that makes any sense?'

'There's something he keeps repeating, but it makes no sense to me. It sounds something like "musical box".'

'Have you got his clothes here?'

'Yes.'

'Could you let me have the keys that were in his pocket?'

'Your friend Julian took them.'

'Where's the nearest telephone?'

'In the office on the right on your way out.'

'Thanks,' I said. 'I'll be back in ten minutes.'

*   *   *

Julian was annoyed when I telephoned.

'I'm in the middle of a conference. Unless it's urgent ring me back in twenty minutes.'

'That might be too late. Please tell me just one thing.'

'All right. But make it quick.'

'Where are the keys to the antique shop?'

'Right there. One of my men is searching the place.'

'Thanks,' I said and rang off.

Julian's car was still waiting outside, so I drove in it to the antique shop. The door was locked. I rang the bell and stood in front of the window so that I could be seen from inside. I was about to ring again when the door was unlocked. I walked quickly into the shop, and the door was closed behind me. I turned and saw a thin man in a tightly fitting grey worsted suit. He had a large nose and a pert, rosebud mouth. I had met him in Julian's office. He was a cipher-clerk in the British Legation, and he knew about my job.

'Hasn't the old girl who owns this place come back yet?' I asked.

'No. She won't be back for three days.'

'How do you know?'

He grinned at me.

'I don't,' he said. 'But that's what Mr. Tuke said, and he's usually right.'

I smiled back at him.

'I've come to borrow a musical box,' I said. 'I don't suppose there'll be any objection. I'll have it sent back tomorrow.'

'Has it got something to do with the case?'

'Yes.'

'Which one is it?'

I pointed to the large ebony box.

'I looked in that one. But I couldn't find anything.'

'There was nothing you could find.'

91

'Then I don't see why . . .'

'It will be back tomorrow,' I said, picking up the box. 'Tuke will see to it himself.'

'So long as it's not my responsibility.'

'Don't worry. You can blame it all on me,' I said.

He looked uncertain, but he unlocked the door, and I carried the box out of the shop and put it in the car.

*　　　*　　　*

Jim was asleep when I came in. Dorothy left me sitting beside his bed. Perhaps it was only the musical box that had persuaded her that I had no questions to ask him. I sat on a light green chair staring at his bandaged head and his bandaged hands lying outside the bedcover as if he were wearing white boxing-gloves, listening to his uneven, gasping breaths, watching his chest rise and fall under the striped flannel pyjamas they had given him. The bandages covered all his head and the upper half of his forehead, but apart from a bruise on his cheek his face was undamaged. And in the same way that I had read the paper in the waiting-room to stop myself thinking, so now I studied his face. I observed without interest that his thick eyebrows met above the bridge of his fleshy nose, his mouth was unusually wide and curled up at the ends, there was an old scar with two stitches in it on his chin where perhaps he had fallen as a child. But even as I examined the texture of his pale skin and the shape of his lips, I could not stop one thought from invading my mind. What had been the purpose of his life? Had he ever known any happiness?

I tried to see him as a child shouting with excitement as the carriage swooped down the switchback, laughing wildly at the clown at the circus, leaping forward triumphantly over the muddy grass to score a goal, diving with his friends into the chlorinated water of the blue-painted corporation swimming-bath. I tried to imagine him with his hair slicked back greasily over his head, swaggering into a bar in Singapore with a group of matelots, standing drinks to the girls and winking at his friends with whom later he would swing home singing dirty songs out of tune. I tried to see him on leave in London, rolling round the pubs with his 'Oppo', cheerful and careless.

But nothing he had told me the previous night fitted into such a picture. He had made few friends—and none of them permanent. He had preferred to remain alone. 'I wanted to work things out for myself,' he said. 'I didn't mind how long it took. I knew I'd find it one day.'

And now as I looked down at him, however hard I tried, I could only see him as someone lonely and bewildered, plodding forward patiently towards a grail he was convinced must exist for him somewhere. But he trusted neither in God nor in Man. He had made a journey without any maps through a barren territory; he had set his course towards Communism because it was the only beacon on a flat landscape.

He moaned and turned his head. Then, slowly, he opened his eyes and stared at me—without recognition. His lips were beginning to move. I leaned forward to hear what he was trying to say. But already from the movement of his lips I knew the two words he was now repeating over and over again, and I walked to the table and opened the ebony lid. The indicator was already set, the motor wound. I pressed down the lever, and, as the spiked brass roller turned, the metal prongs picked out the worn chorale.

I went back to my chair beside his bed, hoping that through the haze of dope and pain he could hear the tune he wanted. His lips had stopped moving and he was gazing vacantly at the ceiling. Then I saw a tear form in the corner of his right eye and slide down his cheek, and I knew the music had reached him.

Suddenly he looked up and recognised me. He stared at me as if he would never take his eyes off me. But there was no anger in his expression—only a kind of perplexed grief. Then he turned his head away. The music ended with a click and a rattle. There was silence in the room except for his heavy breathing. Presently he began to speak. His words came slowly and painfully but they were very clear.

'At first, I thought they were being kind just because they liked me,' he said. 'But I soon found out—even while I was still only a kid—they all wanted something out of me in the end, every bloody one of them. Something of one kind or the other. It came to much the same. They never gave for nothing. Not one of them.'

He was turning his head gradually towards me.

'But I thought you were different,' he said. 'I thought you felt the same way as I did. I thought you wanted much the same kind of world. I thought you wanted to help me because you were real fond of me. That's why I trusted you. That's why I told you the whole works. I should have known better. I should have known you were just like the rest of them.'

He leaned back exhausted. His face was damp with sweat.

'Jim,' I said. 'Jim, please listen.'

'No,' he muttered. 'Not now. Just give me the music and let me sleep. I don't want to know.'

I walked over to the ebony box and wound the motor and pressed the lever, and once again the thin notes dropped into the bare, immaculate room, and once again I sat down by the bed. His breathing seemed to have become fainter and quicker; his eyes were open and they were glazed. I thought he would die soon. I stretched out my hand for the bell, then I decided to wait. If the music still reached him I did not wish to interrupt. And what good could Dorothy do now—except wipe the sweat off his face, which I could do, though perhaps not as gently?

The tune ticked over leisurely and tinkled gracefully to its appointed end. Another click and a rattle—and there was silence in the room. I could no longer hear his breathing, but I could see his chest still moving slightly. I took hold of his right wrist above the bandage and held it. I felt that he should not leave the world without any human contact, and even mine might be better than none.

Suddenly with a frantic shuddering effort he raised his bandaged left hand from the bed-cover and laid it on top of mine and turned his head towards me.

'Why?' he asked with a hoarse cry of despair. 'What made you do it, Tommy?'

Then his head flopped sideways onto the pillow. In my dazed horror I remember that I noticed three flecks of foam on his lips, and I knew that I ought to wipe them away. But I could no longer move. I was still staring down at his mouth when Dorothy came in.

He died an hour later.

*   *   *

I have drunk some whisky, but I must be careful. The hardest part of my explanation still lies ahead—because what happened in Tangier had many consequences, and I am uncertain which I should deal with first—those that affected my mind or those that landed me here, writing in this book to save my skin. Probably I should try to explain things in the order they happened.

*   *   *

I did not want to see Julian that day. I needed time to think. So I sent his car back to the office and walked away from the town towards a little hill called the Charf. I knew that the blowsy Spanish woman who ran a small restaurant near the summit would not bother me, and with a leaden sky there would be few tourists, though it was quite warm.

I sat outside on a wooden bench drinking coffee. To the south I could see the outline of the Riff Mountains, crisp and jagged as if they had been cut from paper. To the north I could see the harbour and Gibraltar like a grey hulk beyond. I tried to forget the tinkling music and the rasping sighs. I knew I must face my own problems. I was alive, and I was in despair near to madness, for I now realised beyond any doubt that during my bouts of amnesia I did in fact change into Tommy.

During the years of my illness I had read sufficient textbooks on psychiatry to understand a little about what is called 'dissociation of personality'. I knew that two (or more) personalities, each of different character, could inhabit the same body. One of the personalities might be aware of all the activities of the other, might be watching him constantly, the other—generally the so-called primary personality—was in many cases prevented from knowing what went on when the secondary character appeared on the stage by periods of complete amnesia. Sometimes the psychiatrists found it possible to combine the two characters into a third person who was, as it were, whole. Or so they said.

I knew, I repeat, about dissociation. But just as we

97

can read equably about cancer yet shudder when we feel a gnawing pain, so now I felt sick with horror. Two persons lived in my body—two so alike that a casual observer could not tell the difference, yet for all that two distinct people, each with his own thoughts, tastes and prejudices, his own passions and ideals, his own vices and temperament, even his own name. I was prevented by my black-outs from knowing anything definite about Tommy. Was he, in his turn, only conscious of what happened to his body when he took the stage? Or was he now at this very moment, as I watched the watery sun break through the clouds, aware of everything I was thinking, of the movement of my hand as I put down my cup? Could he in any way possess the power to influence my actions? From the objective standpoint of psychopathology—how close was I now to certifiable madness?

My hands were shaking, and I locked them firmly together. For three months in the Hospital for Head Injuries, each time I was allowed out I had been made to carry in my breast pocket an envelope with 'Please Open' marked on it. Inside were instructions that if I lost consciousness I should be taken back to Doctor Wilson, who was looking after me. I had known then the fear of going mad, and it was then that I had made the decision to conceal and cheat and lie—to do anything rather than risk being confined as a lunatic—for all the wisdom and kindness of the doctors. For I was convinced from watching them deal with other patients that as yet their science could only cope with one small part of the problem of a shattered personality. Their success depended on the damage having occurred within the small coastal strip they had explored. But beyond lay the vast continent of the human personality about which they could only conjecture in the vaguest terms. And what if my two selves lay beyond their reckoning? I would remain imprisoned while they probed and charted and took fresh bearings. At least I, Peter, was at present free, and I had been in control for over two years. Why should I admit 'abnormalities' which might 'lead to certification', as the books put it?

So, even as I clenched my hands together, I made my decisions. That night I would send letters to Maddern and to Julian resigning my job, for by any standard I was unfit to carry on. I could give two excuses: I found the work distasteful, and I wanted more time for writing. Next, I would not tell anyone about my disability—not even Michael Moylan, who was my oldest friend. Thirdly, I would give up drinking spirits and stick to beer or wine, because I noticed that Tommy took control more easily when I was drunk. Lastly, if only by inference, I would try to find out what I could about my other self.

But what did I know about Tommy? I had probably created his personality by my own wishful thinking; his character could not be different in any obvious way from mine; I knew that he had somehow helped Ageyle and he had gained Jim's confidence. What else? His vaguely felt presence had comforted me during my childhood. I had ceased to be aware of him when I was

99

sixteen. Perhaps that could provide some clue. I tried
to recollect the last occasion on which I had turned to
his invisible being for reassurance. And as the sun
dipped below the horizon and the lights began to appear
like stars, first down in the harbour and the medina,
then in the modern town and lastly on the mountain
road opposite, I did remember, and my mind lurched
back into the past.

*   *   *

The pedals were stiffer than at school, there were
only two manuals and far fewer stops, and the organ
wasn't even electric. But provided I could find Stan
Lakin, who pumped the bellows for two shillings an
hour, and so long as there wasn't a service or choir
practice, I could play whenever I liked. Whereas at
our own parish church, St. Mary's at Little Gritling,
two miles nearer home, the Vicar only allowed me to
play for one hour a week—and then only under the
supervision of his peevish organist.

At first I thought that the presence of Stan Lakin,
concealed behind a purple arras near the vestry, heav-
ing like a Titan at the old-fashioned bellows, would
disturb me. After all, he was eighteen—two years older
than I was. But Mr. Agnew, the Vicar, reassured me.
Stan's parents were perfectly well off, he said. But Stan
was weak in the head, and he didn't mind pumping the
bellows because he liked the sound of an organ.

I slid my fingers into the concluding major chord of F and managed to press the correct pedal with my foot, and looked at my watch. I had been practising for one hour and fifty minutes. In ten minutes' time I must stop because I only had four shillings in my pocket. My parents could easily have afforded to give me a special allowance for my organ practice. But they disliked Mr. Agnew: they thought—quite wrongly—that he was High Church, merely because (probably from absent-mindedness) he had bowed rather frequently to the Altar during the only service they had attended at St. John's.

I closed the book of exercises, pulled out all the stops and let rip for three minutes with broad, imposing major chords and hauntingly plaintive minor ones. Then, to give Stan a rest before the full-blast performance of Handel's Largo, with which I always ended, I played a little hymn tune that I had composed in the music-room at school that term. I used only a plain diapason, to consume less air. As I finished a voice from the aisle of the church said:

'What was that hymn?'

I turned and saw Mr. Agnew. I had not heard him come in. He must have been well over sixty, with thin white hair and a face that reminded one of the stone saints outside the church that had been worn away by the rain and wind. His features were blunt and indistinct. He was almost ugly, but there was a warm kindness I could feel whenever I met him.

'Good evening, Mr. Agnew,' I said. 'Well, as a matter of fact, I wrote it.'

'Did you now? I thought I'd never heard it before. Do you mind playing it again?'

I was delighted to—even though it might mean sacrificing my Largo. I pulled out the tremolo stop for effect and played the tune again. When I had finished playing he said: 'The tremolo doesn't improve it. But I like the tune very much—very much indeed. Could you attend choir practice tomorrow?'

'Yes, I think so, sir.'

'If you've no objection, I'd like my choir to sing it as an anthem the Sunday after next. I know words that will fit perfectly. I shall play it through to them to-morrow evening to teach them the tune. But I want to make sure I get it right.'

I was so excited I could only just speak.

'Thank you, sir,' I managed to say.

'Seven o'clock then,' he said, as he walked out. 'Good night, Peter; good night, Stan.'

In a daze I closed the shutter that rolled down over the manuals and thanked Stan and paid him—I think I may have shaken his hand, because I felt in a way that he was my collaborator—and hurried out of the church. My parents made me change for dinner, and I did not want to annoy them by being late.

As I raced home on my bicycle, my heart was full of pride and happiness. I had always wanted to be a composer; I would persuade my parents to let me leave school at seventeen and study music in Vienna, as my friend Michael Moylan had done. Wild visions swung into my mind as the lane curved and dipped its way through the hay-fields. The dappled keyboard glittered beneath my poised hands, the strings had enunciated the opening theme, I was watching the conductor's baton, and as the beat came my hands crashed out the first heavy chords of my concerto; the dressing-room was full of people, cameras flashed as my hands were clasped and shaken; suddenly the crowd divided, and there stood Penelope in a shining white evening dress, her hands stretched out towards me.

The scene faded as a hay-cart rumbled towards me. I glanced at my watch. I was going to be late. I pedalled feverishly.

My parents had started eating when I reached the dining-room.

'Good evening,' I said, and sat down at my usual place between them.

My father took out his gold watch and flicked open the lid.

'You are five minutes late,' he said.

'And darling, your tie's crooked,' my mother added. 'And did you have a bath?'

'No.'

'Civilised people bathe before dinner,' my father said. 'Where have you been?'

'At St. John's.'

'Why?'

'I practise the organ there. I told you.'

'What a hideous little church!' my mother said.

'It's Norman.'

'I know, darling.'

'Hard as you may find it to believe, your mother *does know* about church architecture.'

'I only meant . . .'

'And had you wished to be accurate you should have said that the church *was* Norman—before the Victorian vandals restored and ruined it,' my father concluded, smiling at my mother across the four early Georgian candlesticks.

I decided I would keep my important news until the end of the meal.

As Jenkins was handing round coffee, I spoke.

'Can I have high-tea tomorrow and skip dinner?'

'Of course you can, darling. But why?'

'Well, actually Mr. Agnew wants me to attend choir practice tomorrow at seven.'

'Choir practice? But your voice broke ages ago and you've sounded like a corn-crake ever since.'

'He doesn't want me to sing.'

'Then what does he want?'

'Well, actually . . .'

'Peter,' my father began.

'You see . . .'

'Will you kindly allow me to speak?'

'Sorry.'

'I have told you time and again that it is the sign of a second-rate mind to sprinkle your every sentence with stock phrases such as "well actually" or "as a matter of fact". Now then. Please tell us what you want to say directly, without meaningless verbiage.'

I stared down at my empty coffee-cup. I reminded

myself that I was sixteen; I was no longer a child; I
could find a job as a waiter in a hotel or I could go to
sea; I could look after myself. But I still felt the tears
of anger and humiliation pricking my eyelids.

'It's nothing really,' I muttered.

'Tell us what you were going to say and let us judge.
Why does Agnew want you to attend choir practice?'

'Because I've written a hymn.'

'Indeed! Can you recite it to us?'

'Well . . . I mean, I haven't written the words, I've
written the tune.'

'Without any words?'

'Yes. Mr. Agnew says he can find words to fit.'

'And he wants you to play your little tune to his
choir?'

'No. I think he'll play it himself.'

'Is there no organist?'

'Yes. But Miss Gaunt isn't as good as he is.'

'Presumably you mean from the standpoint of
technique,' my mother said, laughing.

My father smiled at her affectionately, then turned
back to me.

'Why should Agnew trouble to play your tune to his
choir?' he asked.

'Because he wants them to sing it as an anthem next
Sunday week.'

My mother clapped her hands together.

'How distinguished!' she cried. 'Congratulations, my
little Mozart!'

Then she saw my father's face and her smile faded.

'I think it impertinence of Agnew to arrange this without even consulting us,' he said. 'Our name is involved, and his doting folly may make us the laughing-stock of the entire village.'

'But Evelyn . . .'

'You realise that one of his motives is to get us back into his church?'

'Does that matter? We need only go once.'

'To be ridiculed because of an old man's whim?'

'But the tune may be very good.'

'My dear Mary, what do you suppose Peter knows about composition?'

'His report last term was quite enthusiastic.'

'For his piano-playing, not his composition.'

'But he's had lessons. Haven't you, Peter?'

'Yes.'

'Mary, just ask yourself how much a music master at a public school knows about the most complicated of all arts. Do you suppose that if he could write a symphony, one sonata even, any real musician would listen all day to a lot of young dolts hammering out mazurkas?'

'I've had an idea,' my mother said. 'Why doesn't Peter play us the tune so we can judge for ourselves?'

My father put down his coffee-cup.

'Let us hear it by all means,' he said and rose to open the door for my mother.

*   *   *

106

The old upright piano was still in the nursery. We walked up the oak staircase in silence. I went in and switched on the lights, my parents sat down in the wicker armchairs on either side of the empty grate, I sat down at the yellow, stained keyboard of the piano and began to play my hymn. But even as I played the first few chords I knew that I was lost. The jangling, tinny notes were out of tune; the hammers on middle C and F sharp were broken; the dampers were faulty. The tune sounded very different from what I had played in the peace of the church. When I had finished there was silence.

'I think it's charming,' my mother said. 'But I can't quite see how it could be sung.'

My father threw his cigarette into the grate.

'You play the chords most impressively,' he said. 'I had no idea that you had made such progress.'

He paused, and for one delirious moment I thought that at last I had done something to please him.

'But I'm afraid that I must agree with your mother,' he continued. 'There is no tune at all.'

'But there *is*,' I insisted. 'Only it's my fault for not bringing it out.'

'You believe there is a tune a choir could sing un-accompanied?'

'Yes, I do.'

'Could you sing us the refrain yourself?'

'Yes.'

'Unaccompanied by the imposing chords?'

'Yes.'

'Then your audience awaits you.'

'I've got no words.'

'When I was young we just sang "Lah, lah-la, lah" like that,' my mother hummed, with an encouraging smile.

'Very well.'

'We're listening, darling.'

While I sang the tune I tried to forget them both sitting there without moving in the wicker chairs; I tried to think of the choir in surplices and the congregation listening devoutly as the music rose to the vaulted roof. But it was useless. I had started off in too high a key and I had to begin again in a lower one. I could hear my untrained, rather husky voice trembling from nervousness and cracking on the high notes. I broke off half-way through.

'Please finish it, darling.'

'I can't.'

My father took a Turkish cigarette out of his gold case and lit it, examining the process carefully, as if he had never smoked a cigarette before.

'And are you aware of the reason *why* you can't finish it?' he asked.

'My voice isn't up to it.'

My father watched the smoke he had exhaled spiralling past the noughts and crosses I had scrawled years ago on the wall.

'I'm afraid that it not the only reason,' he said in his quiet, reasonable voice. 'The most important reason still remains to be expressed, and it is this. The tune— such as it is—does not lend itself to the human voice.'

He turned to my mother, who had taken out one of her earlier novels from the bookcase and was reading furtively.

'And I'm certain that you agree with me, Mary,' he said, with a slight frown at her.

My mother put down the book and turned to me with a sigh.

'Darling, you must admit the tune isn't precisely inspiring.' Then, seeing my despondency, she tried to make a joke of it.

'I mean one can hardly imagine the early Christians chanting it as they strode across the Forum towards the ravening lions.'

'You haven't even heard it properly. If only you'd let me play it to you in the church.'

'But I'd love to hear you play it on the organ. You know I would.'

'We'd both welcome the chance of appreciating your progress,' my father said. 'But so far as the hymn is concerned you must confess that we've given you every chance, Peter. And we are both of us agreed. You have assembled a series of pleasant chords, but you have not composed any tune at all. I am sorry, Peter. But in the morning I must ask you to inform that poor senile crock Agnew that his choir will not perform your hymn the Sunday after next or at any other time.'

He got up from his chair, and with a courteous gesture that barely concealed the command, he placed his hand beneath my mother's elbow as if to assist her from her chair. She rose quickly, and together they moved towards the door. As they went out, my mother made a little grimace at me to indicate her disappointment and blew me a kiss.

*   *   *

The next morning I telephoned Mr. Agnew, but the deaf old housekeeper who looked after him bellowed that he had left for the church. It was a fine day, and I had nothing better to do, so I bicycled across to St. John's.

The church door was open, and even as I reached the lych-gate I could hear the soft notes of the organ playing my tune. I crept up the aisle. Mr. Agnew was sitting at the console, his head raised yet inclined to one side, listening to the quiet, reedy notes filling the little church. He was using the upper manual to pick out the melody, and he had made several improvements to the tune itself. Listening to it now, I knew that despite what they said I had written a tune as good, if not better, than dozens of other hymn-tunes that were droned out on Sundays.

When he had come to the end Mr. Agnew turned and saw me and waved his hand cheerfully towards the pew where I was sitting.

'I've been all morning learning it,' he said. 'Stan has got quite impatient with me. But I think I've now got it right, don't you?'

'Yes, sir.'

'I hope you don't mind the small changes I've made.'

'I think they're fine.'

'I wasn't expecting you until this evening, you know.'

'Mr. Agnew . . .'

'But now you're here perhaps you'd like to listen to the chorale we're doing this next Sunday.'

'The reason I came . . .'

But he did not hear me. He had already started playing a Bach chorale. It was 'Jesu, joy of man's desiring'. And as the quietly lilting but steady notes struck and echoed from the whitewashed walls, I knew that Tommy was close to me: he had come once again to comfort me, and I waited for him to speak.

'There's no need to tell him,' a voice seemed to say quietly in my head.

'I must.'

'Why?'

'I said I would.'

'What does that matter?'

'Besides, if the choir practised it, they'd find out.'

'By then it might be too late to stop it.'

'They'd never trust me again.'

'You mean your father wouldn't. Your mother wouldn't mind at all so long as *he* didn't know. And I wouldn't be surprised if he didn't have to go back to London for a fortnight tomorrow.'

'Why should he?'

'His specialist lives in London, doesn't he?'

'I don't understand.'

'I love that tune of yours. Please don't tell Agnew. It'll only hurt the old boy.'

'What else can I do?'

'Take a risk for once, and to hell with them.'

'You don't have to live with them. I do.'

'If only you'd stand up to them—just for once.'

'If only I could! But I'm not tough like you are.'

'You could be if you gave yourself the chance.'

'Never.'

'You could. Listen, Peter. You'll say nothing to the old boy, and you'll go straight back home and tell them that it's your tune, and you intend to have it performed.'

'No, Tommy. I can't.'

'This time you're going to take my advice.'

'I can't, I tell you.'

'If you won't listen to a word I say, there's not much point in me coming to you, is there?'

'Please, Tommy . . .'

'Well, *is* there?'

'I'd feel lost without you.'

'Then take my advice.'

'No.'

'If you don't take my advice this time, I'll leave you. And I might never come back again. And then you'd be sorry.'

'Tommy, do be reasonable. In a year or two I shall go abroad and be free at last. It's not long to wait.'

'You don't like me. You don't need me any more. You just want to be rid of me.'

'You know that's not true.'

'You haven't needed me for almost a year.'

'I suppose that's because I'm growing up.'

'You see? What did I say? You don't really like me now. You've begun to disapprove of me. You only use me now to bolster yourself up.'

'Please . . .'

'Well, just remember this. You may not like me, but I'll always be fond of you, and one day if you really need me I'll come back to you, I promise you.

'So long, Peter.'

'Please come back,' I said. 'Please.'

But already I knew he had gone.

The chorale had finished. Mr. Agnew was walking down the aisle towards me. He looked worried.

'You look ill, my dear boy,' he said. 'Can I do anything to help?'

'It's nothing.'

'Would you like a glass of water?'

'I'm all right, sir. But there's something I have to let you know,' I said. Then I told him of my parents' decision.

And I never heard Tommy's voice again.

*　　　*　　　*

I shivered. It was getting cold on the Charf. I left the terrace and walked into the drab little bar with its sepia prints and old posters and ordered a coffee.

While I waited, I rehearsed my last conversation with Tommy, which I had reconstructed from memory as carefully as I could. Two things were now clear to me. First, I knew why I had blacked out in the antique shop: the chorale had revived bitter memories and had been the cue for Tommy to appear on the stage. Secondly, though it was true that my amnesia after I saw Ken staggering towards me was 'a well-known psychological defence to ward off intolerably painful feelings'—as the text-books said—there might be something more to it than that. For I had been told that, in spite of my head injury, I had, during the few minutes after the dive-bombing, performed various actions, given various orders, before I fainted. At that moment of unbearable anguish was it possible that Tommy had kept his word and had come back to me again? Was Tommy still my friend? If so, I had little to fear. Perhaps even now he was watching over me protectively as he had done when I was a child. But my character had changed with the years: I was less diffident and emotional, less sensitive and more callous. What if Tommy's character had changed even more than mine had? What if he had become tougher, more violent?

It was late. I drank down my coffee, paid my bill and asked the Spanish woman to telephone for a taxi. But —as so often happened—the telephone was out of order, so I walked briskly down the hillside. Though straggling wisps of cloud were drifting across the moon, I could see the road clearly. I picked up a taxi on the outskirts of town. The road stopped two hundred yards short of Madame Badin's villa. I paid off the taxi outside the mosque and clambered down the steep, twisting path that led to the back entrance.

As I turned the corner I saw the man spring at me from out of the shadows. There was a short club in his hand. I raised my arm to stave off the attack. At that moment the other man must have crept up behind me. I felt the blow on the back of my head, and I lost consciousness.

*　　　*　　　*

I was lying in bed, and a woman was bending over me. Then with a surge of thankfulness I recognised Dorothy's wizened face in the light of the bedside lamp. She was peering down at me anxiously.

'Hullo!' I said.

'Now you're perfectly all right. Just lie back and relax.'

But a ghastly thought lurched over me. They might have put me in the room where Jim had died. I turned my bandaged, aching head and looked round. With a sigh of relief I saw the bright flower pictures in cherry-wood frames, the Chippendale chairs with their faded covers, the floral pattern on the drawn chintz curtains.

'Don't fuss,' Dorothy said. 'You're in my spare room. I wouldn't let them take you to that nursing home. I can look after you far better in my own place.'

'Thanks,' I said. I was still half-dazed. 'What's the time?'

'Three in the morning.'

'How long have I been here?'

'Five hours.'

'How badly have . . .'

'There's nothing to write home about. You've had a nasty knock on the back of your head. But that's about all. You were lucky Julian's man appeared when he did. He was waiting for you by the mosque, of course. It serves you right for going off like that without telling anyone. How do you feel now?'

'Pretty bloody.'

'Well, apart from mild concussion, Doctor Scott can find nothing wrong with you *physically*.'

'What do you mean by that?'

'We were afraid you'd gone out of your mind. For hours you were raving like a lunatic. Thank heavens you've come back to your senses. We were getting quite worried.'

'Who is "we"?'

'Julian, Doctor Scott and I.'

'Julian's been here?'

'He only left an hour ago. He'll be back in the morning. Now swallow this luminal in a little water, and we'll both try to get some sleep.'

'I'm sorry to have been such a nuisance. Thanks for all you've done.'

'Nonsense. That's what I'm here for. Now there's a pot under the bedside table, and you can switch out the lamp for yourself. If there's anything you want, just tinkle the bell. I'm only next door and I'm a light sleeper.'

'I really am grateful.'

'Forget it.'

At the door she paused and turned.

'Peter, just tell me one thing. What have you got against Julian? Why do you dislike him so much?'

I felt suddenly afraid, for I now knew who it was that had been raving.

'I don't,' I said.

'Never mind. Perhaps you'll tell me one day,' Dorothy said, and the door closed behind her.

*   *   *

I awoke the following morning feeling no more discomfort than I would have had with a bad hangover. But Dorothy insisted on bringing me breakfast in bed.

'After concussion you must lie quiet for a time,' she said firmly.

Julian arrived soon after eleven. He was wearing a light grey flannel suit, an Old Wykehamist tie and a pale blue shirt that matched the colour of his watery eyes. His receding, grey-flecked hair fell over his collar behind his neck so that it looked as if he were wearing a wig that had slipped backwards. When he spoke I could see that whatever had been said last night he was now determined to be pleasant.

117

'How do you feel?' he asked brightly.

'Far better.'

'Last night we were quite concerned about you.'

'Julian, can I meet the man who saved me? I'd like to thank him.'

'*Il est debout devant toi*,' Julian said. 'You behold him with your very eyes.'

'I know, Julian. And I'm really grateful to you. But I'd like to meet the actual man who drove them off.'

'You mean my agent?'

'Yes.'

Julian picked up an ash-tray, sat down in an arm-chair beside the bed and lit a cigarette.

'I don't think that would be possible,' he said. 'You'll appreciate that I like preserving my agent's anonymity.'

'I see.'

'I'm sure you understand.'

'Did your agent recognise either of the men who attacked me?'

'Yes. They were two toughs from the water-front—not even members of the Party. Incidentally, Silva was arrested by our French friends in Rabat at nine this morning.'

'Good.'

Julian stroked the edge of the ash-tray with his bony fingers.

'You know, you said some pretty wild things last night,' he said.

'Did I?'

'Of course I realise that you were concussed. All the same, some of the lunatic things you came out with revealed quite a strange state of affairs in your subconscious.'

'I can hardly be expected to control that,' I said smiling.

Julian frowned.

'At times it was hard to tell where your allegiance lay.'

'Poppycock.'

'You ranted like a parlour red.'

'Look, Julian, if you're trying to suggest that I'm a Communist in disguise, I must tell you that I reckon that you're the one who's lunatic.'

Julian winced with annoyance.

'I don't need to be taught my job,' he said. 'I know your position in the spectrum of political and social thought as well as you do. But I must tell you, quite frankly, that I'm disturbed by the unresolved conflicts in your subconscious which were displayed so openly last night.'

'You don't think I'm a good security risk?'

'I didn't say that. But if you ask me—no, I don't. Not until I've had a psychiatrist's report. Sorry. But there it is.'

'You needn't feel sorry, Julian. You see, I'd already decided to chuck the job.'

He looked at me for a while in silence.

'When did you make that decision?'

'Last night on the Charf.'

'What will you do?'

'Finish my travel book and try to get a job as foreign correspondent on some paper.'

Julian stubbed out his cigarette.

'You won't forget the Official Secrets Act, will you?'

'No, I won't forget.'

He got up and smiled at me politely.

'We shall miss you,' he said. 'But I think your decision is wise. I've long suspected that you lacked the right temperament for the job. But Maddern always thinks he knows best. We shall have to inform him of your decision, of course. I can send him a signal this afternoon.'

'Please do.'

'I presume you won't stay on out here.'

'No. I'm tired of the place. I shall leave for London tomorrow.'

Julian nodded his head like a bird pecking at seed.

'Again I think you're wise.'

He moved vaguely towards the door.

'Well, I suppose I should be going,' he said.

'Just one thing, Julian. Why were they so certain that I was the person who had found out about the ship from Jim?'

He stared at me.

'But Silva couldn't help knowing.'

'Why?'

'You weren't drunk. You must remember.'

'Remember what?'

'Has the concussion affected your brain? You can't have forgotten. What game are you playing?'

'Forgotten *what*, for Christ's sake?'

'At a quarter to seven that morning Jim telephoned from the antique shop to Silva, who came round immediately. He was in the shop with you for the last hour before you left—as you and I both know perfectly well.'

I made an attempt to cover my mistake.

'Yes, but even so . . .' I began.

'But even so,' he cut in, 'I confess that I found it odd that you said nothing about his visit when you came to see me the following morning. However, your information concerning Mustapha was so urgent that I decided the other matter could wait. You didn't know then that the shop was being watched. Why didn't you tell me that Silva had been there? Why did you pretend just now that you had forgotten about his visit? Why?'

'If you want to know the truth, I *was* drunk, and I had a black-out.'

Julian examined my face as if he were reading the contours on a map.

'You weren't drunk when you left,' he said. 'I'm afraid I don't believe you.'

My head was throbbing and I felt desperately tired. I made the mistake of losing my temper.

'I don't give a damn if you believe me or not,' I said. 'I'm sick to death of you and the whole organisation. Thank God I've finished with the lot of you.'

Julian cocked his head on one side and raised his

eyebrows. Then, looking at me with deliberate calm, he shrugged his shoulders and turned round slowly and left the room.

* * *

Skimming quickly through the pages that I have written I realise that I may have given the impression of a solitary person wandering almost friendless through thirty years of life. This is because my report has been mainly concerned with the period when I was travelling in Arab lands, and—apart from Edward— few of my friends were in the Middle East at that time. Admittedly, I did not make friends easily when I was at school—Michael Moylan was the only one who lasted. But when, after a year in Vienna during which I learned many things about life but not much about the piano, I came up to Cambridge, I blossomed out. To my great surprise I became quite popular for a while. And though I lost touch with them during the two years in London immediately before the war when I was studying for the Bar, I ran into several old friends in the Hotel Cecil in Alexandria or in Shepheard's when we were on leave from the Western Desert, and I made new friends in my regiment.

I mention this to show that I was not a recluse. I should add—to make this section complete—that my mother had been killed in an air-raid in 1940 and my father had died of pneumonia in 1945. I had an aunt living in Dorking and an uncle living in Bournemouth, but we seldom met, for I did not care for them—nor they for me.

I realise now that I should have told at least one of my friends about my condition. But I felt as morbidly embarrassed to display my weakness as I might have been to pull open my shirt and reveal a livid growth. And now I have almost left it until too late. Why did I not have the sense to tell Michael Moylan and his wife Pam that first evening in London when I dined with them on my return from Morocco? But Michael talked about the music he was writing for a film, Pam talked about her research work at Chatham House, I told stories about cigarette smugglers in Tangier, and the evening slipped by pleasantly in their house in Halsey Street. I could so easily have confided in them then— over the last glass of port. Instead, I asked them to help me find a small flat in Chelsea. And in their kindness they found me one. A week later I was installed in a furnished flat above a garage in a fairly quiet mews, and I settled down to finish my travel book. And as the weeks passed by I found that I could even forget about Tommy for a whole day. If only I had used my time *then* for writing this statement! But how was I to know what would happen?

*   *   *

The first incident in London that disturbed me took

place outside the Travellers' Club. I had been lunching with David Evans, who had been Adjutant to the Crendon Yeomanry when I joined. As he was saying goodbye to me at the main door, a staff car drew up and General Maddern got out and walked quickly up the steps towards us. I did not even know that he was in London. I was standing in front of the door so I moved aside. And he passed me—without even a faint hint of recognition. But I was certain he had seen me.

'He's in the hell of a hurry, isn't he?' David said, laughing to cover my embarrassment. 'Perhaps he's left his dispatch-case crammed full of secrets in the bar.'

'Or perhaps he's been lunching with his teetotal wife and can't wait for a double,' I suggested.

But I was worried. Maddern had replied most politely to my letter of resignation. Why should he suddenly decide to cut me?

The second incident occurred at noon a week later. I was walking past the Ritz when I met Edward Pratt. He was wearing lemon-coloured suede boots, a bright check suit and a foulard tie. He looked as if he had just left Newmarket.

'My dear man, I've just been to the most boring conference,' he said. 'For heaven's sake let's nip downstairs to the bar and have a quick one.'

'What are you and Maddern doing back in London?' I asked when we had settled down with our drinks.

'Haven't you heard? My dear man, it's been one of the greatest scandals for years. It's rocked the War

124

Office, scared M.I.5 out of such wits as they've got, and given the Foreign Office a fit.'

'What happened?'

'We were rumbled, that's what happened. The whole organisation has been blown sky high.'

'But how?'

'A full-page article in *Al Misri*—quite obviously Government inspired.'

'I can't believe it.'

'It gave the whole works—establishment figures, information centres, names of agents—yes, your name was mentioned—details of operations and future plans —the lot. Of course our Embassy people were in a rage. Up till then they hadn't realised the extent to which we were poaching on what they reckoned was their own territory. The Ambassador was on to the Foreign Secretary before you could say "Pratt". There was the hell of a stink, and we were ordered to remove ourselves elsewhere.'

'When did this happen?'

'About a fortnight ago.'

'So you're operating from London.'

'As best we can. But it's not quite the same thing.'

'Did Maddern tell you he'd seen me?'

'No. But he was awfully disappointed when you resigned. You were his top blue-eyed boy. In fact he seriously considered trying to make you change your mind. He'd even drafted a letter. But he tore it up, I don't know why. Have you done anything in this lurid town to blot your copy-book?'

'Not that I know of.'

'Incidentally, what were you doing striding down Queen's Gate at three o'clock yesterday morning?'

'I wasn't. I've been working flat out on my travel book. I've been in bed every night by eleven—and sober what's more.'

'Don't try and kid your old uncle. I was coming back from a dance in a taxi and I saw you clearly. I shouted and waved at you. But you took no notice at all. Have you got a bint in Queen's Gate?'

'I wish I had!'

'Oh well! Give me her address if you get tired of her. Now I must run. So long, Peter.'

*   *   *

I was worried. Why had Maddern torn up the letter he had drafted? Why had he changed his mind? One possible explanation was too ghastly to contemplate, and until I had any reason to believe that it could be true I refused to consider it.

The full horror of my situation did not strike me until I discovered that my flat was being watched.

The floor above the large garage opposite had been converted into two flats with separate entrances. I knew that the one farthest away from me was to let, because I had looked over it. A few days after my conversation with Edward I noticed early one evening that the flat was occupied. The red curtains were drawn aside. For an instant I saw a man's thin face looking out. Then the curtains were twitched back into place again. Later that evening I saw a thin, tall man shutting the blue-painted door behind him. The following morning at ten, as I went out to do some shopping, I noticed another man opening the door with a latch-key. He too was tall and thin. He looked so much like his companion that for a moment I could not spot any obvious difference. Then I saw that his face was slightly less angular and his hair appeared to be shorter. I decided that two middle-aged men, perhaps brothers, had taken the flat, and I thought no more about it—until I became aware that they were seldom in the flat together. One of them would leave shortly after the other had returned. And each time I left my flat I could see the shape of a man standing close to the muslin curtains that permanently covered the window. There was no doubt about it: they were taking it in turns to watch my flat.

I wondered if I was now being followed, but I could detect no signs of it. Certainly the two thin men never moved out in pursuit of me. I knew that I should now confess my problem to Michael and his wife, or even to Edward. But I still hesitated. Then, three days later, I made a discovery that forced me to take action.

For the past three weeks I had woken up feeling tired. I attributed this to my obvious worries and to the strain of finishing my book in a hurry; for my publishers were getting impatient—they wanted to produce the book before the situation in the Middle East altered and my views became stale.

One morning after I had just woken up, as I walked across to the small bathroom, I happened to look at the light grey suit I had worn the previous day. I had folded the trousers across the back of one chair and hung up the coat on another, because there was no hanging cupboard in the flat. I now noticed that the lower half of the trouser legs seemed darker in colour. I bent down and touched them. They were wet. I looked at my overcoat hanging on the back of the door. It was drenched with rain. But the previous day had been dry, and I had stayed in all evening. I drew aside the curtains. Rain was falling steadily from a leaden sky. Then I knew what had happened and I understood why I woke up exhausted each morning and why Edward had seen me striding down Queen's Gate. Tommy had begun to take over control while I slept. I had reached the last stage before certifiable lunacy.

I felt the saliva flooding into my mouth. I rushed into the bathroom and was sick. Then I plunged my head into a basin of cold water. And even as I dried my face by the bathroom window I saw the tall, thin shape behind the muslin opposite. I went back into the living-room and got back into bed. But though I shut my eyes I could feel the walls of the room closing in on me. I no longer felt competent to take any decision about my predicament; I only knew that unless I got away from London I would go mad.

I swallowed a grain of sodium amytal and took deep breaths until I felt calmer. Then I dialled Michael's number. Pam answered the telephone.

'Michael's just decanted himself to the studio,' she said. 'And I'm drinking black coffee to brace myself for historical research. We invited two film tycoons to dine with us last night. They drank Vichy water while we got plastered from sheer nerves. How's your great work progressing?'

This gave me the cue I wanted.

'Don't I seem to remember that you once had some place in the country?'

'I'd hardly call it a place. You mean The Dump. Two rooms and a leaky roof. We've still got it. Why?'

'Could I rent it?'

'Rent it! My dear Peter, wait till you see the place. It's just a broken-down cottage at the end of a desolate lane. You're welcome to it any time you like. But I don't advise it in winter.'

'I must get away from London to finish my book.'

'It's certainly quiet enough, and I daresay you could persuade Mrs. Bain to come out from the village and cook you a meal at mid-day. But she'd want to be gone before it gets dark. And you'll be freezing cold, and if it rains you'll be drowned.'

'Could I really go there?'

'If you're prepared to rough it, I don't see why not.'

'Where is it?'

'On the Sussex downs. Five miles from Hassocks.'

'Could I go there tomorrow?'

'There's nothing in the cottage. You'll have to take your own food and drink.'

'Pam, I'm terribly grateful.'

129

'Wait until you see The Dump. Our other name for it is "Moylan's folly". Why he ever *thought* he could work down there I can't imagine. The place is so damp we can't even install a piano. I'm warning you, Peter. It's pretty grim in winter.'

'Tomorrow's Friday. Would either of you be in if I came round to see you about eleven?'

'So far as I know, we'll both be in all morning. Drop in for a drink and we'll give you the keys and incidentally the address, which might be a help. See you tomorrow.'

'Thanks enormously.'

'Look out your woollies,' she said, and put down the receiver.

I could not work that day. I managed to pass the remaining hours of the morning by packing, telephoning to cancel the few appointments I had for the next fortnight and buying tins of food from the grocer's shop round the corner. After lunch I took another sodium amytal capsule and slept for an hour. Then I walked up the King's Road to the local cinema. I sat close to the door in a gangway seat in case the unreasoning impulse to get out into the open overwhelmed me, and I tried to concentrate on the film, which was set in Hollywood.

I realise now that this was an insanely stupid way of spending my last day in London—when disaster was already rumbling on the horizon and must soon, almost inevitably, crash over me. I should have appreciated then that I would need a solicitor and all the help from my friends I could get. Perhaps 'insanely' is the right word, for I felt dull and tired, incapable of action yet curiously light-headed. I believe I know what a rabbit feels, caught in the headlights of an approaching car.

I must set down carefully my movements during the rest of the evening. At seven-thirty I drank a pint of bitter in the Six Bells. I returned to the flat about eight and cooked myself supper. At nine I took two luminal tablets and went to bed. I was feeling drowsy; I knew that I would soon go to sleep.

*   *   *

The pictures on the grey walls of the long drawing-room were shifting and flickering in a haze, as if I were watching them through a mirage. I was conscious of intense fear. Some instinct kept me from crying out in my terror.

I was sitting in a yellow armchair by the chimney-piece. To my right, a short, wiry man of about fifty, with wide shoulders and a broad, wrinkled face was sitting on the sofa facing the gas fire. He was wearing a brown tweed suit and slippers. A white silk scarf was tucked into the collar of his open shirt. In the armchair opposite me on the other side of the chimney-piece a heavily-built, plump man was sitting with his legs crossed. His smooth white face looked as if he had recently shaved. There was a cut on the side of his flabby

131

chin. He was wearing a smart pin-stripe suit, a stiff white collar and a polka-dot tie.

Standing in the centre of the group the three of us made was a boy of about seventeen in jeans and a polo-necked sweater. In the cold light of the chandelier above him his face looked worn and tired, but he was slim and quite handsome, with his pale hair and delicate features, and his eyes were shining with excitement. All three of us were now watching him.

'Right, Arthur,' the large plump man said. 'You can begin. First, give us the background you're to use.'

The boy glanced towards him for an instant, then turned to the man on the sofa.

'My name is Arthur Wood,' he said in a quiet, even voice, as if he were repeating a poem he had learned by heart. 'I'm seventeen. I'm on holiday from a secondary school in Reading. The headmaster thinks I may get a scholarship to Cambridge if I work hard enough these next two terms. My father is a foreman at Chiver's biscuit factory. My mother was a schoolmistress, but she now looks after our home. My uncle emigrated to the States when he was a youngster. He made good in the canning business in Chicago. That's why he can afford to pay for my expenses and even give me a dinner-jacket and a complete new outfit. I'm travelling to New York on the *Queen Mary* to spend Christmas with him because although he's married he's got no children and he wants to see a member of his own family. Mother was keen for me to go. I believe she thinks he may leave me something in his will.'

'Good,' the plump man said. 'Carry on.'

Once again the boy's eyes flickered towards him, then returned to the man on the sofa.

'I met Mr. Grant here when he came down to talk to our Sixth Form about the Middle East. I told him that I was interested in politics. I said that if I didn't get my scholarship I'd like to find a job as secretary to some politician. Mr. Grant said the only politician he knew at all well was Lloyd Ashton.'

The boy paused and looked at me slyly. As soon as he spoke the name I could guess what was coming. Ashton was a successful politician who had been for a while in my regiment during the first years of the war. We belonged to the same London club. I had met him once or twice after he had become a junior minister and had found him as friendly as ever. He was a stout, red-faced man with a pleasantly jovial manner which disguised an acute intelligence. He was going to Washington in December to attend yet another international conference. Had there not been rumours about his private life he might well become Prime Minister. Though he was married and had children I knew that he kept a small flat in Pimlico where he entertained his boy-friends.

'Mr. Grant said that Mr. Ashton might be interested in me,' the boy continued. 'He took down my name and address, and said he'd send me a letter of introduction, but I suppose he must have forgotten.'

'So much for the background,' the plump man said. 'Now let's have the approach.'

133

'I don't try to get picked up for the first two days of the voyage,' the boy said in the same flat voice. 'I try to make friends with youngsters of the same age. But I make sure that Mr. Ashton notices me, and I find out which bar he uses. On the third day out, I go to the bar before dinner and sit down near him—next to him if possible—and order a cider. Then I give him the works.'

At that instant the boy's whole personality changed. Suddenly he became alive. The hard look vanished from his eyes, which now looked soft and languid. The tenseness melted away from his body, which now became sinuous and graceful. He took three paces towards the sofa, moving with the charm of a young animal.

'Mr. Ashton,' he said in a voice which was deferential yet quivered with suppressed emotion. 'Mr. Ashton, please forgive me for butting in like this—without being introduced or anything. But we've got a mutual friend, and I'm sure he'd want me to come up to you. Please forgive me if I've done wrong.'

He lowered his eyelashes and smiled shyly and bent his head. It was beautifully done. A shade more emphasis and he would have looked coy—and the effect would have been spoiled.

The man on the sofa unfolded his muscular hands and lit a cigarette.

'Well done,' he said.

The plump man got up and put a flabby hand round the boy's neck and smiled at the man on the sofa.

'Now aren't you glad you let me take him on?' he asked with a smirk of triumph.

The man on the sofa slowly turned his green eyes towards me.

'I'm afraid our friend Tommy still doesn't approve,' he said. His voice was deep, and he spoke with only a faint trace of a foreign accent.

'But after all, no weapon is clean. Even a sword can be rusty.'

While my mind struggled desperately to assemble the stray pieces of knowledge about Tommy that I now had collected, and to arrange them into a coherent picture, I realised that I must exert every muscle, each little bit of cunning, every trick I'd been taught, to avoid giving myself away—if only because at last I had a chance to find out what Tommy had been doing. The man had said: *still* doesn't approve.' This at least was a pointer.

'Do you really think Ashton could be blackmailed?' I asked.

'Arthur's only seventeen,' the plump man said. 'Ashton would get at least two years.'

'Not if he went to the police.'

'George, I appeal to you,' the plump man said, turning away from me with a shrug of his heavy shoulders. 'Can you see a man in Ashton's position going to the police?'

George, as I now knew he was called, flicked away a speck of ash that had fallen on one of the sofa cushions.

'It depends,' he said after a pause. 'Personally, I think it's worth trying.'

'Even if Arthur goes to prison for blackmail?' I asked.

George looked up at Arthur and smiled.

'You're prepared for that, aren't you?' he said in his deep, calm voice.

'I am that,' Arthur replied.

'He's well trained,' the plump man said with a sudden titter.

George grinned at them both affectionately. His squat, uptilted nose above the short upper lip and broad mouth made him look like some impudent urchin who had dressed up in his father's clothes.

'Kenneth,' he said to the plump man, 'why don't you take Arthur down to the dining-room and give him something to eat and drink?' he suggested.

'Arthur can go down by himself. He knows the way.'

'Tommy and I will follow you in two minutes. I'd just like a few words alone with him.'

'Right,' Kenneth said. 'Don't be too long. Arthur and I want to get home.'

'Don't worry,' George called out as they left the room. 'I'll send you back in the car. You'll be home within an hour.'

When he turned back to me, George was still smiling.

'What's wrong with you tonight?' he asked.

'I'm tired, I suppose.'

'Why did you try to frighten that boy?'

'Surely you admit that it was safer to warn him in advance?'

136

'Isn't that for me to decide? And why has your attitude been so different tonight? For the first time I can sense a definite hostility.'

'You're quite wrong.'

'No, Tommy. I am not wrong. I have an extra sense that has often saved me.'

He got up and stood with his back to the chimney-piece.

'Listen to me carefully,' he said. 'You came to us out of the blue with a letter from our friends in Cairo. You say that you are a journalist who has worked on the side for British Intelligence, and the letter from the Ikhwan supports the fact. I still wonder if you are not playing a double game. But then you give us the most important information we have had this year. You give us a full and accurate report on the secret organisation of your Middle East Bureau. You provide this information free—without asking for one penny—which makes me suspicious. But I realise that your people would never make such a great sacrifice to plant you amongst us. No. I decide that you are a genuine idealist.'

He paused and lit a cigarette. His eyes never moved from my face.

'Then you tell us that you have come from Tangier,' he continued. 'But you can give us no information about the arrest of Silva and his subsequent so-called "suicide" in the cell of a French prison in Rabat. You say this had occurred after you left. However, I notice that you react strongly when I speak of the young sailor they were forced to get rid of. You say you had only met him once. But we have since discovered that you were in the nursing home with him when he died. And again tonight I notice that our use of the young boy disturbed you. And then I begin to wonder—and I am still wondering—if for all your apparent boldness and determination there does not lie some fatal streak of sentimentality in your nature that utterly destroys your resolve. I am still wondering why you should have stayed with the young sailor till he died. I am still wondering why you should have been so evasive about Silva, who was in fact arrested the day, or rather the night *before* you left. Unfortunately, the report he was about to hand in was captured with him, and he was a proud man who liked to work alone.'

George crossed the room and stood by the side of my chair gazing down at me.

'However, his report may not be lost. Because we have just heard that before they killed him he managed to communicate with a Frenchman who for a time was in the cell next to his. This Frenchman was released yesterday. He arrives in London tomorrow at noon. I would like you to be here at one o'clock to meet him.'

I forced myself to look up steadily into his green eyes.

'I'll see you at one o'clock,' I said.

I got up from my chair.

'Would you like a drink or would you rather go straight home?'

'As I told you, I'm tired. I think I'd better turn in.'

He was watching me carefully.

'Perhaps you're right,' he said. 'You know your way out, don't you?'

'I do. Good night.'

'Good night, Tommy.'

I could feel his eyes following me as I walked slowly out of the room.

I hurried down a flight of thickly carpeted stairs into a dark, green-painted hall. The door on the left led presumably to the dining-room. Three overcoats were lying on a polished oak refectory table. I picked up my coat, opened the front door and walked out into the misty night. I was in Queen's Gate.

*　　　*　　　*

I have only one hour left. I must hurry. I haven't time to set down the thoughts that churned round in my mind that night as I hurried home. I write 'that night'—because so much has happened since then and each hour has seemed longer than a day. But, in fact, the scene that I have described took place in between two and three o'clock this very morning.

I need only say this: I realised that as soon as the Frenchman reached London, the man called George would presume that Tommy was playing a double game, for obviously Silva would have reported that it was Tommy who had betrayed Jim's confidence. I had yet one more reason for leaving London.

I reached my flat at about half-past three. I took two luminals and went to sleep.

I was awakened by the telephone ringing. I looked at my watch. It was ten o'clock. I stretched out for the receiver. As I answered the 'phone I heard the noise of the button being pressed in a call-box.

'Peter?'

'Yes. Speaking.'

'Now listen carefully. Don't say my name, but can you recognise my voice?'

I was silent for a moment. The voice was disguised, but I was almost certain that it was Edward Pratt.

'I think so,' I said.

'Can you give me a clue so that I'm sure you've guessed right?'

'Yes. Daiquiris and Alice.'

I was thinking of the two Brigadiers he called 'Tweedledum and Tweedledee'.

'Right,' the voice said. 'Now this is urgent. You remember the spot where we last met?'

'Yes.'

'I'll meet you there at eleven-thirty sharp. All right?'

'I'll be there.'

'Good,' he said, and put down the receiver.

At twenty-five minutes past eleven the taxi I had picked up in the King's Road—after making sure that I was not being followed—arrived outside the Ritz. It was raining. Edward Pratt was waiting on the pavement. When he saw me inside the taxi he opened the door quickly and got in and slid back the glass screen behind the driver.

'Trafalgar Square, please,' he said.

Then he closed the screen and leaned back.

'Sorry to make such a fuss,' he said. 'But I'm afraid things are pretty grim. Hence all these precautions. You're not being followed, but I'm almost certain that your line is tapped.'

He looked at me sharply.

'Does that surprise you?' he asked.

'No.'

'Just what have you done?'

'I'm not sure.'

'Don't be a fool. We've no time to waste. Can't you see I'm trying to help you?'

'First, tell me what you know. Then I swear to God I'll tell you all I can.'

'You realise that if it's found out that I've warned you, I'll be court-martialled?'

'Yes, I do. I'm grateful, Edward.'

'I don't know the full details. I only heard by chance this morning. You're in trouble, Peter. M.I.5 are after you. They're getting a warrant this afternoon. You'll be arrested tonight.'

I was silent. At last it had come. Perhaps because in my imagination I had lived through this moment so often during the last few days my only emotion now was one of relief.

'Why don't you say something? Why don't you protest? Why don't you tell me it's preposterous? Peter, I just can't believe that you can have . . .'

'How long have you got?' I asked.

'I'm meeting Maddern at twelve. I don't want him to suspect . . . I daren't be late. This was the only moment I could get away.'

'Where are you meeting him?'

'In the War Office.'

I leaned forward and asked the driver to go down Whitehall and drive round St. James's Park. Then I closed the glass screen, and while the taxi slithered along the shining street I began for the first time to explain about the black-outs I had had since returning to Cairo. I concluded by telling him of the plan to blackmail Ashton.

Edward listened in silence. The time was five minutes to twelve when I had finished.

'I'll drop you at a rank and take this taxi on,' Edward said. 'Now *you* listen to *me*. First, I believe every word you've said. Secondly, you must find yourself a solicitor and tell him all you've told me—but in far more detail. And you must find one before six o'clock tonight. Have you got a family solicitor?'

'Yes, but he's pretty senile.'

'I could advise you to go to mine. But I just daren't get mixed up in this. You must have friends in London who can get you a first-class man.'

'Yes, I have.'

'Who?'

'Michael Moylan and his wife.'

'Are they in London now?'

'Yes. I could go there right away.'

'Good. They can help you. But don't go back to your

flat until *after* you've seen the solicitor. And for God's sake remember you haven't seen me.'

Edward tapped on the window, and the taxi stopped. I got out and opened the door. It was no longer raining.

'I can never thank you enough,' I said.

'Don't try.' He blinked at me and tried to smile. Then he bent forward. 'Remember we never met today,' he said quietly. 'So long, Peter. Good luck.'

*   *   *

I found Michael and Pam drinking pink gins.

'You wretch!' Michael said. 'We'd almost given you up.'

Pam glanced at me, got up from her chair, and walked across the room and kissed me.

'What's wrong?' she asked.

'Give the poor man a drink first,' Michael said. 'What will it be?'

'Gin and tonic, please.'

'Now then,' Pam said as Michael went to the drink tray. 'Out with it.'

Once again I explained as quickly as I could what had happened to me since I returned to Cairo. I ended by telling them that 'a friend' had warned me I was going to be arrested and had advised me not to return to my flat until I had seen a solicitor.

When I had finished Michael sank down his pink gin

and looked at the clock over the chimney-piece. The time was half-past twelve.

'Oliver Nesbitt is the man for you,' he said. 'Don't you agree, Pam?'

'If we can get him,' she said. 'But his firm is so wildly successful he's seldom free.'

'If I 'phone his office now I might catch him,' Michael said and walked out of the room. .

'I don't suppose you feel much like eating,' Pam said. 'But you'll stay to lunch, won't you?'

'Thanks.'

'Will you forgive me if I go down and see how things are progressing? I don't entirely trust Mrs. Craig with Wiener Schnitzel.'

Pam smiled at me apologetically and went out. I suspect that she wanted to be with Michael while he telephoned. I picked up a Chatham House report and tried to concentrate on the cool, detached sentences.

About ten minutes later Michael returned.

'I think we've got things fairly well taped,' he said. 'At least we've got Oliver. The snag is that he's got to be in Court this afternoon and can't get away until five. But in the meantime he wants you to write down an account of the whole business from Cairo till today with full details. He wants to know how you were wounded, the names of the doctors who looked after you, the hospitals where you were treated, the dates you were there. He wants to know when you started the black-outs, when you first found out about this other personality, how you got mixed up with our Intelligence boys, what happened in Tangier—the lot. He says he doesn't want a formal statement. He just wants you to put it all down in your own words— everything you can think of. And remember you can always afford to tell your solicitor the truth.'

Michael glanced to make sure that my glass was not empty and made himself a pink gin.

'I suggested you should do your writing here. But he thinks that since we're known to be friends it's just possible they might come here for you. He thinks you're safer out of London. So the plan is this. You catch the next train down to Hassocks. From there you can take a taxi to The Dump. Pam would come with you, but it's Mrs. Craig's afternoon off so she's got to look after our brat, and I've got a meeting with my boss at three-thirty. But I shall motor down later with Oliver. We should arrive at The Dump soon after eight. We'll collect you and dine at some pub on the way back to London. Oliver can go through what you've written and ask you questions. He'll then work out a formal statement with you. Then we shall go straight to your flat, and Oliver will telephone to Scotland Yard to say that you have a statement to make. And we'll be with you when they come for you. I think that's the lot. Pam's in the kitchen making sandwiches in case you feel hungry on the train. All you have to do is to stop your taxi on the way to the station and buy yourself a big notebook to write down the whole works. Every detail you can remember, he said. From Cairo until the time we come to collect you.

*   *   *

I have almost finished now. I can risk another small drink.

*   *   *

And there he goes! And I come on again!

Of course, he doesn't know how hard I try to get through the suggestion to him that he needs a drink. After all, that is *one* of the ways I can take over. And really it's kinder than making him remember something- so horrible that he blacks out just because he can't face the memory. Mind you, I don't want to make him an alcoholic. That might kill both of us. But I do need to take over from time to time. After all, I'm as important as he is. This 'secondary personality' business is just cock.

Sometimes he carries on as if he'd created me. But that's not quite true. I was there long before his mother told him those silly Tommy stories. All he did for me was to allow me to develop. He helped me grow. I do grant you that. But when he used to talk to me at night he'd feel I was so close to him and real that I could hold him in my arms, and I did believe that he was honestly fond of me. I'm still sure that while he was a kid we

146

were good friends—though he always disapproved of me. I mean, he thought I went too far. The trouble was that our whole attitudes to life were entirely different. Though there was a lot about his parents— particularly his father—that he resented, he still absorbed a big dose of their pathetically bourgeois morality. He thinks that Vienna and Cambridge and his travels liberated him from their influence; in fact, at heart he's still conventional and resolutely upper-middle class.

Even by the time he was sixteen he'd become a fairly typical public-school product. By then, of course, I'd realised the truth. He wasn't really fond of me; he only called for me when he needed my help. For the rest of the time I could rot, so far as he was concerned. And I admit I was hurt. There I was, watching over him night and day—even when I wasn't summoned— and he just banished me from his life unless things got difficult.

And what had I done wrong, for heaven's sake? On the few occasions I'd been allowed to take over I'd done nothing wicked or cruel or mean. I suppose that one *could* say it was cruel to kick away those wooden chocks, but at least I aimed the roller away from the man's head, and I only did it so that Peter could be happy with Penelope.

No, I must confess that Peter's indifference hurt me deeply, and I told him so that day in church. You see, I was really fond of him—I still am in a way—but I wasn't going to be treated like some slave who appeared to order when the magician rubbed the ring. So I went underground. I was lying 'dormant', as one might say, during his wild days in Vienna and throughout his three years at Cambridge, where I admit I had to exercise great patience and self-control, because at that period he started getting interested in politics.

The poor boy claimed he was a socialist, while, in fact, he was just a woolly-minded liberal. By then it was patently obvious that no political creed except Communism could offer an intelligent man any hope. A classless international society was the world's only chance. At the very worst, we had to choose between the repressive measures of revolution and a second World War. And we could, then, still have determined to a great extent the nature of the revolution towards a new society by determining the nature and principles of the party that would make the revolution. But there was little time left. Yet during this crucial period, while liberal and socialist governments were collapsing all over Europe, Peter decided that the world could only be saved by a conference of the great monopolistic powers at which the unsatisfied powers should be invited to state their grievances and claims—as if they didn't do so already. He made impassioned speeches at the Union, mainly based on pamphlets by Aldous Huxley, in which all the old clichés were paraded. 'The ends are judged by the means,' he proclaimed. 'I shall never fight to defend my country or to uphold my beliefs because violent means are never justified.'

I was enraged. But what could I do? He never called

for me now, and I had no chance to take over. I could only wait. My opportunity didn't come until the second year of the war.

Needless to say, as soon as war was declared Peter's conventional morality triumphed over his religious scruples. Perhaps that isn't quite fair because he enlisted the day after Munich. But it was typical of him and his class only to take action when it was too late. However, he was sent to an O.C.T.U. and early in 1940 he was commissioned and sent to the Crendon Yeomanry, which was then training with tanks on Salisbury Plain.

When the regiment was ordered abroad I reckoned my chance would soon come, for I knew that Peter was too sensitive to endure the full horrors of tank warfare. Sooner or later he'd call for me. And he did—when he'd been hit in the head with shrapnel and his driver's head had been split open. He called for me—and as soon as I appeared he blacked out. He disappeared because he couldn't bear it any longer. He just let me take over—which I did pretty well, considering I hadn't been summoned for nine years. I took over until we were safely in the ambulance and on the way to Tobruk.

But then, as the days in hospital passed by, I realised that the whole situation had changed. He had now started to black out without calling for me. He'd just vanish and leave the stage empty, as it were. All I had to do now was to wait until he'd blacked out and I could take over complete control. For the first time I was able to lead an existence of my own. And I'd got this advantage over him. I knew every single thing that he did; I was there watching him. But his amnesia prevented *him* from finding out what I was up to when I took over.

For instance, when he found those bank notes in his room at Shepheard's he just hadn't got a clue where they could have come from, and he never did understand about Ageyle. But since this notebook is going to be read by Oliver whatnot and I bet by dozens of psychiatrists—because presumably there'll be a trial and they'll be called to give evidence—I'll explain exactly what happened.

He'd blacked out all on his own, without any suggestion from me, that evening in Maddern's house before dinner. He was tired, he was nervous and he'd had a bit to drink. Anyhow, I had to take over, and I reckon I was quite brilliant. I expounded his Fertile Crescent scheme, and I persuaded Maddern to discuss it with that old bore Parry the following morning. When I left the house just before midnight I decided that I'd earned a night out and I was determined to have my fling. So I took a taxi back to Shepheard's and changed out of my dinner-jacket into an old tweed suit. Then I strolled into the streets.

I'd no definite plan, and I made a bet with myself that I'd go wherever the first pimp that accosted me suggested. And that's how I got to know Ageyle. The pimp drove me in a taxi to the outskirts of Giza and introduced me to the fat woman's brothel. She was half French, half Syrian. She had three girls, she said, very young and very special. I said I was interested, we agreed the price, she shouted upstairs, and they appeared. All three of them were naked—except for Ageyle, who wore a small brassière. I think that was why I chose her. Somehow it excited me. Within half an hour I had found out the truth.

I may say that if ever there was a perfect example of the complete futility of your bourgeois liberal it is to be found in *Peter's* behaviour with Ageyle. What in heaven's name was the use of offering her six pounds? Even supposing she could have concealed it from the fat woman, what use would it have been to her? If she had been able to escape where could she have gone? To one of the other big cities? And how long would six pounds have lasted her?

She had been sold to the fat woman by her parents when she was twelve. Of her, one could literally say she had not got one friend in the world. Yet Peter thought he could help by giving her six pounds. And then—after he'd understood about the cigarette burns —the sheer idiocy of rushing straight back into the house! What good did he imagine *that* was going to do? Presumably he didn't suppose the girl stayed there for pleasure. In which case, the two suffragis were obviously there to prevent her escaping, and to prevent anyone else trying to help her get away, come to that. Yet in he charged without even pausing to work things out and got knocked out, of course, and very nearly ruined my careful plan.

Because, you see, I didn't lose my head that first evening in Cairo, when I found out about the cigarette burns and Ibrahim Bey. As I held her in my arms I questioned her gently but persistently to find out as much as I could before making any plan. I found out, for instance, that after Ibrahim had started his experiments on her —and burning was only one of his specialities—she had once managed to escape. The window was not barred then, and she had got out and crawled along a narrow ledge onto a balcony from which she had dropped into the street. She had managed to find her way to Alex, where she tried to find work. But the fat woman with Ibrahim's help and money tracked her down, and she was brought back again.

The afternoon she was brought back the fat woman spent an hour alone with her in her room. I will not describe what she did to Ageyle. Even now it makes me sick to think of it. I will only say that after she had finished with her, the clients could not use Ageyle for a week.

When Ageyle told me about it in quiet little hissing whispers I realised first, that she would be far too afraid to make any statement to the police should I get them to visit the brothel, secondly, that she would never run away again unless she were certain that she could be protected and given permanent security. But how could this be done? She needed money and friends. Suddenly I saw how I could provide her with both. Maddern's indiscretion after dinner might well be her salvation. As Ageyle lay with her arms clasped round me I whispered my plan into her ear. Then I dressed, left her a pound, kissed her goodbye and went downstairs to pay the fat woman.

I made a mental note of the address of the brothel and took a taxi out to Heliopolis and drove to a dingy block of flats where a young married couple I had known in the days before Peter was invalided home used to live. Khalil was Egyptian, his wife Hanouna was Lebanese, and I knew that they both belonged to the Ikhwan Al Muslimin, the revolutionary organisation called the Moslem Brotherhood.

I was lucky. I saw from a card on the peeling door that they still lived there. It was two in the morning. I rang the bell insistently. Inside, a baby started to cry. Then Khalil opened the door and stared out furiously. He was wearing a long white night-shirt and he had not put on his slippers. I noticed that he had hammer toes.

'Khalil!' I said. 'It's Tommy. Do you remember me?' Immediately, the scowl left his face.

'*Ahlan wa sahlan*,' he said. 'Welcome.'

'Can I come in? Sorry to disturb you at this hour. But it's urgent.'

'*Beti, betak, itafadhl adkhal*,' he said. 'My home is yours. Please enter.'

Ten minutes later I had explained to them both about Ageyle.

'But what do you suggest that we should do?' Khalil asked, scratching the side of his long nose with his thin almost simian fingers.

'If there were money, could you arrange for some

153

married couple from your Brethren *outside* this country to look after her?'

'If there were money—yes.'

'Where?'

'We have friends in Khartoum who are both kind and gentle. But they are very poor. They would need money.'

'Could they find her work?'

'In time—yes, I think so.'

'Could you take her down to them.'

'Yes.'

'Khalil, do not be a fool!' Hanouna cried, throwing back her heavily-oiled curls. 'You know that we have no money and three children to feed. You could not even pay for the tickets—let alone pay the bribe to get her into the Sudan without papers.'

'If there were money, when could you go?'

'Not for some time. First, we must write to our friends to ask if they will take the girl.'

'How much money do you reckon we would need? Would two hundred pounds be enough?'

'Yes,' Khalil said slowly. 'That would be enough.'

'I'll come back with the money as soon as I can. But I must go now.'

'*Allah yakarimak*,' he said. 'May Allah bless you.'

I thanked them and left. After walking for ten minutes I picked up a taxi and drove to a certain hotel. I write 'certain hotel' in that tiresomely coy way because I don't want the person I met identified. I'm sick of betrayals and reports and the whole paraphernalia of

Intelligence. It's a dirty business—and that's a fact. I don't want to get yet another person into trouble. Peter doesn't know the man, and he never will. I'd met him in Cairo before Peter was invalided home, when I'd started to lead an independent existence.

My friend was pleased to see me again.

I came straight to the reason for my visit. I told him that I'd dined with General Maddern that night and had got hold of a valuable piece of information. I could see he was interested.

'May I ask what it is?'

'The precise date we intend to evacuate our troops from Cairo and Alex.'

'It would be easy to invent a date. How can I be certain your information is genuine?'

'You can't,' I said. 'You've just got to take a gamble. But work it out for yourself. You can check that I *did* dine with Maddern tonight. You know where my sympathies lie. You know I've taken a risk even by coming here.'

'But why *have* you come here—and at three in the morning? To make me the present of a piece of information? Surely not.'

'No,' I said. 'I've come because I need money.'

'How much?'

'Two hundred pounds.'

'Will the troops be withdrawn into the Canal Zone?'

'Are we agreed?'

'I cannot pay you now. I haven't the cash with me. But the money will be delivered to your room in

Shepheard's tomorrow morning. It is your turn to trust
me.'

'I do,' I said.

'Why?'

'Because if I provide you with one useful piece of
information you have already appreciated that I might
one day provide you with yet another.'

He chuckled. But I knew the money would be paid.

*　　　*　　　*

I walked back to Shepheard's feeling pleased with
myself. I had saved little Ageyle—and at no cost to
Peter. I had written down his appointment with Maddern and Parry at eleven in his engagement book so he
would see it when he woke up. I had been clever and
efficient. I made only one mistake. I did not appreciate
that Peter might leave for Damascus almost immediately. I tried hard to get through during his second day
in Cairo—but without success, which was infuriating,
because, of course, the money had been paid. And the
next day he left for Damascus, so I had to wait until
we returned to Cairo.

Even then things nearly went wrong. He'd blacked
out after dinner at Mena House—the scar on the
suffragi's forehead reminded him of Ken, his tank
driver, and away he went. So I'd gone round to the
brothel to warn Ageyle to be ready to leave the following evening. Khalil and his friends were going to take

156

care of the suffragis, and the rest was easy. I was lying in Ageyle's arms and I must have relaxed control, because suddenly Peter took over—and nearly mucked up everything, as I've already said. But thank heavens he blacked out again the following night from sheer drink. So I took the money from his suitcase and gave it to Khalil, and the operation was carried out successfully—as that bastard Maddern would say. I only wish I could have helped them. But the fat woman would have recognised me, and I didn't want to get Peter involved. Anyhow, little Ageyle is now safe and happy in Khartoum. I only wish Peter would go there, so I could be with her again.

That brings me to a point I'd like any psychiatrist reading through this to consider carefully. I'm just as much alive as Peter is—more so, when you come to think of it, because even when I'm not on the stage I'm aware of what's going on. I, Tommy, have as much right to existence as he has. It is I, Tommy, who am using these fingers to write and these lungs to breathe. Yet I can almost never decide where we should go or what we should do. For instance, why shouldn't I go to Khartoum to see Ageyle? She'll be grown up by now and probably even more beautiful. I'd give anything just for a fortnight with her. You see, I believe she really was a bit attracted to me. And I shall never forget those two sessions we had together. But what chance have I got of seeing her again? Almost none. Why? Because I'm the so-called 'secondary' character—merely due to the fact that I came onto the stage later.

Whichever way you look at it, I swear it's not right. When they begin to cope with our problem—dissociated personality and all that—why should I be the one to be removed? Not that I want Peter suppressed; I'm not saying that. But why can't they merge us in some way? After all, I am fond of him—even if he does disapprove of me. Think *that* one out before you start your tricks.

And it isn't as if I'd ever been a Communist agent—or anything approaching one. I suppose you could describe me as an emotionally convinced fellow-traveller. I must say it makes me laugh when Peter reads books that suggest that the Communists only employ carefully selected agents who have been specially trained and tested over a long period. They'll get their information anywhere—provided they're certain they won't compromise an important source. And I never dealt with the top office. The Syrian and Jim and Silva were all expendable. They'd even ditch George Kärnten if it suited their game. And now that this Frenchman who's been released from the gaol in Rabat has arrived in London, I've had it. They'll get me if they can. That's why I'm so thankful we've left London. At least we're safe down here—unless they had me followed. But I looked round carefully at the station, and I couldn't spot anyone.

Dear Peter is only concerned about the detectives and M.I.5. I'm far more disturbed by the thought that even now one of *their* men may be moving towards this cottage, advancing cautiously step by step along that dark lane. However, Michael and his solicitor friend should be here soon. And then we'll be delivered over to the detectives—and, in time I suppose, to the doctors. Far better that than Jim's fate.

I admit that until the Tangier business I hadn't realised just how ruthless they could be—though I suppose I should have known.

This is what happened. I made great friends with Jim after I had taken over in the antique shop. (Incidentally, I knew as soon as the musical-box started playing that Bach chorale that Peter would black out rather than face the memories the tune brought back.) I had a long talk with Jim. His knowledge of Marxist doctrine was, of course, almost nil. But he was eager and sincere, and he was admirably discreet about his job. Then, as the hours of the night passed by, he began to get drunk. In a pathetic way he was determined to impress me with the importance of his work for the cause. Though I tried to stop him he insisted on telling me every single detail of the *Salomé*'s trip. He even insisted on telephoning Silva to come round to the shop to meet me. By then he was convinced that I could help them in some kind of way.

Soon after Silva arrived, Jim left the room to be sick. While he was away I warned Silva to keep him sober. I said I thought he *might* be indiscreet when he was drunk. That was all that I said.

Then something took place that had never occurred before. I gradually became aware that I was no longer alone on the stage. For the first time, Peter was there watching me. With a sudden stab of fear I saw the danger. He would report all he saw and heard. I said goodbye to them both and left the antique shop immediately.

But when we reached our room up in the villa, I realised that Peter had overheard the most important fact of all—the whole purpose of the *Salomé*'s trip. Jim had given me a piece of notepaper with the shop's address on it. As Peter came round from his black-out, he took this piece of paper and on it he began to write down Mustapha's name and the address where he was in hiding. I struggled with him desperately, but I was losing control. Peter was taking over again. But he was still dazed. He folded the piece of paper and tucked it away in his ticket-pocket. If he had not found it that morning Jim would be alive today. I am certain of that.

But why kill the boy—and why make such a botch of it? What wrong had he done—except to trust a fellow-traveller? And once Peter had given the name and address to that loathsome, cold-blooded monstrosity Julian, the damage was complete and irreparable. Jim's murder served no purpose—except revenge. And I had to watch at his bedside, while Peter sat there, knowing that every word he spoke to Peter was meant for me, knowing that unless I could take over from Peter soon we would meet the same end, because Silva would guess that it was I who had betrayed the secret.

But the assault on me that night was unsuccessful—

though for a while I was so shaken by the pain and shock that when I saw Julian peering over me like a vulture I raved at him. The things I said then started him on the trail that is leading to Peter's arrest. Yet even as I ranted at Julian my own guilt remained. By warning Silva, I had betrayed Jim's confidence. I was as responsible for his death as Peter was. Not only that. By relaxing control in the antique shop and allowing Peter to slide back into the scene, I was directly to blame for Mustapha's arrest. I had let down my friends and the cause I believed in. I was determined to make up for it when I got back to London. And I did.

I told that grinning ape George Kärnten every detail about Peter's organisation. I admit that it gave me pleasure to think of all the trouble I was stirring up for Maddern and that vulture in Tangier. Each piece of information I gave to George, each time I attended a meeting in his house reduced my feeling of guilt. And I could attend his meetings quite often when they were late enough, for I'd found out that by an intense effort of will I could now take over while Peter slept. I can use the stock phrase quite literally and say that this gave me a new lease of life.

Then, at one of the late sessions, George sprang on me his plan to make use of a seventeen-year-old Cockney boy who'd been adopted when he was thirteen by a queer hanger-on of George's called Kenneth. For the last four years the boy had been dosed with Marx and Sade in about equal proportions. If ever one could say that a boy had been perverted, Arthur had. I had been brought into the affair because my name—or rather Peter's name, for they imagined that 'Tommy' was only a nickname I used with my comrades—Peter's name, I repeat, was to be used by the boy in effecting his approach to Ashton.

I reckoned the whole plan stank from every point of view. For a start, I didn't believe it would work. Ashton was far too experienced and astute to allow himself to be blackmailed. Secondly, I was sorry for Arthur. I couldn't bear to see the way that fat white slug Kenneth pawed him and ordered him about. The boy was more like a ventriloquist's doll than a human being. The utterly submissive way he would turn towards that plump, greasy, flabby man made me sick. I was arguing fiercely against the plan when I was conscious of the same feeling that I'd experienced in the antique shop. Peter was shifting back onto the scene. I was losing control. A minute later—and he'd taken over.

I reckon that after the arrest at least *some* psychiatrists are bound to read these pages. To help them I'll say this. We know how and why I take over from Peter—head injury combined with protective amnesia which leaves the stage free for me. But we don't know why *Peter* should suddenly take over from *me* in the middle of a scene—when according to the books he shouldn't come round till the following morning. Well, I reckon I've worked out a theory that explains the reason for it. Each time it's happened, *we've both of us felt the same way*. We were both of us wildly attracted to Ageyle. We were both of us fond of Jim and worried about him. We were both of us revolted by the way they were using Arthur.

Now, if I'm right it means there's some hope—because during these last few years, instead of agreeing with Peter less, I've found myself in agreement with him more often. He got it all wrong up on the Charf when he imagined that over the years I'd got more violent. Paradoxically enough it was when Peter brushed aside his scruples and took to violence that I first became disillusioned with it. During the years in the desert I saw what it really meant to use force. I saw the shell crash against the turret. I heard the men screaming as they were burned alive. And I learned that toughness wasn't as important as I supposed. The tough ones were often much less use than the mild, rather sensitive types like Peter. Then, during these last few years, I've had a taste of what it's like to use force in so-called peace-time. I shall never forget the expression in Jim's eyes when he asked: 'What made you do it, Tommy?'

Don't make any mistake. I still believe in Communism. I still believe that a classless international society based on a common love of humanity is the only hope for our race. But I don't believe it can be achieved by force.

While Peter's been writing in this book I've had time to work things out. I reckon that just as the simple teachings of Christ were distorted by fanatical converts, so the simple doctrines of Communism have been distorted by disciples ranging from Stalin to Kärnten. 'Power corrupts,' said Acton. 'Absolute power corrupts absolutely.'

Perhaps there will always be prophets who go into the wilderness and discover truth and come back to the cities to preach it. Perhaps their disciples will always misunderstand their message, because they're tempted by power and confused by the quick returns one can get by force. Perhaps violence will always triumph—until the whole tribe perishes as the world grows cold and falls into an infinity of space.

I haven't drawn the curtains so that I shall be able to see the lights of their car turning into the lane. It's a clear night. Some of the stars I'm looking at must be hundreds of light-years away. Set against that distant background, set against the present condition of the world today, with millions in prison, millions in fear and want, what does it matter what happens to me? Of what importance am I, Tommy, as I wait in this whitewashed room? I'm not even a complete unit in the myriad. And I wonder . . . the police or friends, the killers or even an ambulance—does it really matter which comes up the lane?

*   *   *

I have read through these pages from beginning to end. I have read all that Peter has written and all that Tommy has written. The jigsaw is complete. I am neither Peter nor Tommy. But I now understand. . . .

The car has not yet arrived. I could still try to get abroad and escape both the detectives and George Kärnten and his friends. But I shall wait here until Michael Moylan and the solicitor arrive.

I know that I shall be arrested when we get back to London, and I dread it. I dread the imprisonment, the questions and the trial.

But I believe that I can face whatever ordeal may lie ahead. For at last I am whole.

AUTHOR'S NOTE

I was wounded in the head in the Western Desert. I worked for the Middle East Intelligence Centre. I have been in several hospitals for head injuries. I have suffered from 'black-outs'. I was in Cairo frequently during the years immediately after the war. I have made use of my own personal experience; I have even used two incidents from my travel books, word for word. But all the characters in my novel are imaginary, and imaginary names have been invented to suit them. If by any chance I have used the name of a living person I can only apologise.

Maugham, *Hon.* **Robert Cecil Romer,** 1916–
    The man with two shadows ₍by₎ Robin Maugham.
New York, Harper ₍1959, °1958₎

   165 p.   22 cm.

   ɪ. Title.

PZ3.M4415Man2   823.914   59–8249 ‡

Library of Congress